PRAISE FOR

Drawing Outside the Lines

"This is a simple and splendidly constructed story, history, and inspiration at a human scale. Susan Austin expertly weaves together fact and educated conjecture into a memorable tapestry of the formative years of a remarkable woman."

—STEVEN FINACOM, Past President,
Berkeley Architectural Heritage Association

∞∞∞∞∞∞∞∞∞∞∞∞∞∞

"*Drawing Outside the Lines* opens a window into another time and place. The rich descriptions of life in Oakland, California in the early 20th century presents readers with a window into the remarkable life of Julia Morgan who challenged gender discrimination to follow her dream of becoming an architect. The added bonus is the rich historical backdrop carefully researched and presented through the imagined story of Morgan's early life. Readers will find mirrors in Julia's story as she describes wanting something different—something that doesn't fit the norms of the time and place. This wonderful story encourages us to take a stand and follow our dreams—it is indeed a story for our time—one of inspiration and perseverance. A must read!"

—MARGIT E. MCGUIRE PhD,
Former President of National Council for the Social Studies

∞∞∞∞∞∞∞∞∞∞∞∞∞∞

"Austin imagines Julia Morgan's life with authority. She makes an important historical figure accessible to us . . . [and] makes us see and feel what Morgan was up against, which makes her spectacular work all the more impressive."

—GENNIFER CHOLDENKO, author of
Al Capone Does My Shirts

◇◇◇◇◇◇◇◇◇◇◇◇◇◇◇◇◇◇◇

"A compelling story with a wealth of evocative details offers a memorable telling. Woven into the story are Julia Morgan's ability, persistence, and ambition . . . an inspiration for any reader."

—JOAN SCHOETTLER, author of
Ruth Asawa: A Sculpting Life

◇◇◇◇◇◇◇◇◇◇◇◇◇◇◇◇◇◇◇

"Susan Austin's deep research makes her imagined story of Julia Morgan's early life and influences plausible—possibly even more accurate than some of the biographies out there. But Austin's passion for the subject of this trailblazing architect makes the story fun and inspiring."

—KAREN MCNEILL, PhD, author of
Parisian Foundations: Julia Morgan at the
Ecole des Beaux-Arts, 1896-1902

Drawing Outside the Lines

A Julia Morgan Novel

Susan J. Austin

Published by SparkPress, a BookSparks imprint,
A division of SparkPoint Studio, LLC
Phoenix, Arizona, USA, 85007
www.gosparkpress.com

Published 2022
Printed in the United States of America
Print ISBN: 978-1-68463-159-9
E-ISBN: 978-1-68463-160-5

Library of Congress Control Number: 2022913049

Interior design by Tabitha Lahr
Drawings on pages vii, 49, and 209 by Suzanna Klein

For kids of all ages
with big dreams

Part I
The Flame

Julia's Oakland Home

Chapter 1

FROM OAKLAND
TO BROOKLYN

As the train leaves the station, I watch Papa grow smaller. When he's no more than a tiny dot, I lean back in my seat, thinking about my good luck. Instead of being stuck at home with my baby brother, Sam, and annoying big brother, Parmelee, I'm on my way to New York.

I pull my books from the green satchel then stack them on the table in front of our seat. Scrutinizing the pile, I slip my favorite on top. Emma, my younger sister, wrinkles her nose. "Eww! How could you?"

I rest my hand protectively on the arithmetic book. Emma and I are so different. She brought her embroidery without being reminded. I deliberately "forgot" mine. She spent days choosing her travel clothes, while I finished in less than an hour.

Mama sits across from us, trying to stop my brother Avery from playing with his first loose tooth. A hopeless task.

As we roll by the shimmering San Francisco Bay, I tingle thinking about my secret—the real reason why I had to be on this train. Mama must never find out. She has strong feelings about what is best for me. Going on this trip was not on her list.

When I begged to go, she scowled. "It's about duty," she said. "The sooner you accept this, the better. It's time you learn about managing a household, Dudu."

As the eldest daughter and almost twelve, I hear this often. And yes, my family calls me "Dudu." That's Parmelee's fault. When he was little, he couldn't say Julia. "Dudu" is what came out. The name stuck, but I don't mind.

I had nearly given up hope of being on this train. Mama seldom takes my side. If I told her the real reason I had to come along, it would make matters worse. In desperation, I used my strongest argument. "I can keep Grandmother happy while you pack her things."

Here I was on firm ground. Mama was truly worried about Grandmother's fragile nerves. And Grandmother's move from New York to our house in Oakland would no doubt get her riled up. Waiting for Mama's answer, I held my breath. When she nodded a silent yes, I remembered to thank her before racing upstairs to pack.

Two days later, I'm on the train, trying not to fidget. Mama doesn't approve of fidgeting. Because I have taken this trip several times before, I know what to expect.

Bedtime is my favorite part, when the porter performs his magic trick—turning our passenger car with its benches and tables into an enchanting sleeping car. A few quick maneuvers and the cushioned benches become a bottom bed. With the release of a latch, a second bed drops from the ceiling. The porter rests a stepladder on the upper-bed rail. For his last trick, he lets loose the ceiling-to-floor curtains that turn the double-decker beds into a cozy hideaway.

The next morning, Avery and Emma begin pleading with me to read them a story.

"Just one, Dudu. Please?" Avery begs.

"Pleeeze," Emma says, clasping her hands together.

"My word! You two are pests."

"Pleeeze," they whine together.

"All right. Just one. And only if there's a place to sit."

"How good of you, Dudu," Mama says, pulling her latest project from her knitting basket. "I'll enjoy the peace and quiet."

"Come on, you two. Lead the way."

Using a wide stance with our arms outstretched—a good practice to keep us steady when the train tracks curve—we stagger to the parlor car. It's a cozy place. The dark mahogany chairs and comfy sofas are already filled with passengers. Gas lamps glow under delicate glass shades painted with tiny blue and purple flowers.

Fortunately, one small sofa is empty. I take my place in the middle. Emma rests her head on one shoulder, and Avery's on my other side, fiddling with his loose tooth.

Over the next few days, the train chugs closer to New York and to my secret. The wheels on the track keep reminding me. *Almost there, almost there*, they sing over and over. To pass the time, I take my chessboard to the parlor car, where I can usually find someone to play who doesn't mind losing.

When we finally pull into the Chicago station, Mama supervises transferring our baggage to the overnight train for New York.

"No wandering away. Do you hear?" she warns.

Emma and I grab Avery's hands. The cavernous hall with its dome-like ceiling is home to more tracks than I can see. Trains constantly stream in and out. People rush by, heading in different directions.

When Mama is satisfied that our trunks are safely stowed on the right train, she sighs. Papa usually sees to such matters. Clutching Avery's hand, she scrutinizes Emma and me. "Stay close," she orders.

As we make our way through the crowds, the unthinkable happens. We lose Avery. It takes only a second. A speck of dust lands in Mama's eye. She releases his hand to pull a hankie from her dress sleeve. And poof! Avery vanishes as if tapped by a magic wand.

Mama's face pales like she is about to faint. Papa would know what to do, but he isn't here.

"Sit there," I order Mama and Emma, pointing to an empty bench. "Don't move. I'll be back."

Mama protests, dabbing a hankie to her damp forehead. "But Dudu. I don't think…"

"I'll find him. Stay here."

I have no idea where to look, but a single thought runs through my head. *Think like Avery. Think like Avery. A little boy, loose in a train station.* Where would he go? Haven't I learned anything from living with three brothers?

And then I know. Locate a locomotive, and I'm sure to find the scamp.

Presto! I easily spot the seven-year-old boy in his navy and white sailor suit, his straw hat slightly off-kilter. He's statue-still, gazing up at an enormous engine belching black smoke from its stack. I march him back to the bench, his small hand firmly clasped in mine.

A day later, when we pull into New York City's chaotic station, I'm the first off and into our waiting horse-drawn carriage. My face is warm, my palms sweaty. I pretend to be counting our luggage so that Mama doesn't notice my state of excitement. In a few minutes I shall get my first glimpse of something so spectacular I fear my heart may stop.

Chapter 2

PIERRE LeBRUN,
THE ARCHITECT

In the past, traveling from the train station to my
grandmother's house meant ferrying across the East River
to Brooklyn. Not today. Today we will ride our carriage
across the magnificent new one-of-a-kind Brooklyn Bridge.
Four weeks ago, on May 24, 1883, the bridge opened for
business with bands playing and flags flapping. Now I will
see it for myself.

I know all about the Brooklyn Bridge. Papa and I
pored over every Oakland newspaper article we could
find, each cut out and pasted in my thickening scrapbook.
As our carriage nears the bridge, I lean over the side for a
better look. Mama pulls me back by my waist, but I see
it clearly. Its two gigantic towers, and the colossal cables
that hold everything up. My heart thumps in time with
the horse's hooves.

With barely a bump we roll onto the bridge's road reserved for carriages and animals. The cows and goats hardly slow us. I spot the raised pedestrian walkway in the middle of the bridge. A girl my age leans against its railing, staring down at us. I wave to her. She reminds me of Mary McLean, my best friend, who like Mama, didn't want me to go on this trip, but for different reasons. "What if the bridge falls down?" she cried.

To my disappointment, the ride across ends too quickly. Minutes later our carriage stops in front of 51 Remsen Street, Grandmother's four-story brownstone where Mama and my Aunt Julia grew up.

From the start, my grandmother works herself into a tizzy, wanting a say about everything placed inside the mover's crates, and insisting on touching every item left behind. Strands of white hair work loose from her tightly wrapped bun. "I can't do without it," she murmurs, clutching a vase.

Our days are so busy with packing Grandmother's things that we have not returned to the bridge. Still, I find sly ways to remind Mama. I'll say, "I wonder how many people can walk over it at once?" Or, "How long do you think they'll leave the celebration flags on the towers?"

Mama acts as if she doesn't hear me. With each passing day my agony increases. Is it possible I will never set foot on my beloved bridge? In desperation, I begin planning ways to sneak out of the house.

Then one morning a messenger boy arrives at the door. I pay little attention until Mama opens the envelope and starts reading.

"Oh, isn't that nice," she says.

"What, Mama?"

"Cousin Lucy and her husband, Pierre, have invited us for a stroll on the new bridge. Your Aunt Julia, too. You remember Cousin Lucy, don't you?"

"When, Mama? When are we going?" I ask, pressing my hands together to keep from snatching the letter.

"Why, Dudu. We're much too busy for such a frivolous outing. What could you be thinking?"

My jaw drops.

"Close your mouth, young lady. Don't let the flies in."

"But Mama! This is the most miraculous engineering project ever—the longest suspension bridge in the world. People from all over the world are coming to see it. I don't know how you..."

Mama cuts me off. "Duty first. How many times do I have to tell you? Besides, we've already seen the bridge. And we'll see it again when we leave with Grandmother."

"But Mama . . . "

Grandmother thumps the tip of her cane on the floor. "Eliza. Don't be silly," she says to Mama. "This is a lovely invitation. You must take the children. All work and no play. Tsk. Tsk. No, I insist you go."

I want to hug my sweet grandmother but instead I bring Mama her writing paper. As she writes *Dear Cousin Lucy*, I wonder how I will be able to wait.

It's finally Saturday afternoon, and I've been ready for hours, boots shined and buttoned. My frilly white dress is Mama's choice. An oversized light-blue bow is tied low on my waist, fluffed up to look like a small bustle in back. Corkscrew curls, fresh from the horrid curling iron, reach my shoulders. A straw bonnet trimmed with a matching blue bow rests atop my sketchbook.

This sketchbook isn't the one I used four years ago during that gloomy visit to Grandmother's. Sitting by the parlor window, memories of that ghastly time are vivid. I quiet my mind in my usual manner. First, I organize my colored pastels from light to dark. The clock in the hallway ticks loudly, but the sound fades as I become lost in my drawing.

I begin sketching pictures of those sick days: Emma with diphtheria, me with scarlet fever, and then poor Emma sick again, this time with scarlet fever. Mama said we looked as red as cooked lobsters. I touch that hard place behind my ear, where excruciating pain sent me back to bed just when I was feeling better. The doctor warned Mama those earaches could return. He was right—they do.

I finish with a picture of me riding Parmelee's new velocipede, a gift from Aunt Julia. Big and red, it has two small wheels in the back and a big one in the front. My love affair with the contraption ended when Parm tried to run me down on the sidewalk.

As I print *Six Frightful Months* on top of my drawing, Emma and Avery find me.

"Play with us," they demand together.

Emma clutches her box of pick-up-sticks. She knows I seldom turn down a game.

"One game. That's all," I warn, concentrating on the front door.

Sliding the lid off the box, I shake out the colored sticks. Avery goes first. His pick makes the pile of sticks jiggle. When it's my turn, I reach for the red stick when

Emma asks me a surprising question. "Dudu, do you remember when you told us about the man who built the Brooklyn Bridge? Mr. Roebling?"

"Uh-huh." Slowly, I free the red stick from the pile.

"Did he have scarlet fever like us?"

I'm surprised that Emma is also thinking about those dark days. "You remember that Mr. Roebling was sick? Good for you. He was sick for years, much, much longer than us."

Outside, carriage wheels squeal. A horse whinnies. Cousin Lucy and her husband, Cousin Pierre, have arrived. Whenever my parents mention this man, they always say "Pierre LeBrun, the architect." Remarkably, Cousin LeBrun's father and brother are also architects.

"Children. Stop staring out the window," Mama scolds. "Where *are* your manners?"

When the door opens, Emma, Avery, and I are lined up to greet our guests.

I'm dazzled by the elegant couple, especially Cousin Pierre with his high-top hat. Cousin Lucy in her summer-whites hugs each of us, leaving behind a trail of rose-scented perfume. Although my curtsy is acceptable, a sudden shyness turns my voice into a whisper.

The day is warm and sunny, and the sidewalks are crowded. Everyone is headed to the same place: the bridge. When we reach the corner, I spot the one of the two towers. With every step, more and more of this engineering marvel is revealed in all its glory.

Chapter 3

BELOVED BRIDGE

As soon as my foot touches the bridge, I stifle the urge to run to the far end and back. Mama is watching. Instead, I stand on my toes, looking upward, my arms outstretched. I turn around once, slowly, then a second time. Blood pulses in my ears like the waves crashing against the base of the towers.

"Amazing, isn't it?" Cousin Pierre says, his head tilted like mine.

His simple question unleashes a torrent of thoughts.

"I can see them now, the cables."

"Go on," he urged.

"I know how they were made, but actually seeing them makes everything clear."

"You know about the strands and wires?"

"I do."

Papa and I had gone over every detail. I know about the miles and miles of long wires, no fatter than a pencil. I know about how they are wrapped tightly together into thick strands, and how the strands are then wrapped into the enormous cables.

Cousin Pierre's dark eyes sparkle in the sunlight. "Let's see then. How many wires are in a strand?"

Papa once asked me the same question. But now Cousin Pierre, the architect, wants to know.

"Two hundred and seventy-eight," I answer with certainty.

He nods. "Now, here's a tough one. How many strands in a cable?"

"Nineteen," I shoot back, looking up at the enormous cables, each the size of a gigantic tree trunk.

"Good. So how many wires did Roebling need for his four cables?" He looks at me. "You know who Roebling is, don't you?"

"Oh, yes, sir. The chief engineer." My mind races as I do the calculation, one Papa and I never made. Closing my eyes, I imagine standing in front of the blackboard, chalk in hand. Cousin Pierre waits. In the time it takes three seagulls to circle a tower I have my answer. "Five thousand, two hundred and eighty-two, plus a few more for extra strength."

"You know about those?"

"Yes, sir! Papa and I know how Roebling added extra wire because of some poor material."

"Good for you," he laughs. "Now, let's put your sketchbook to use."

As I draw parts of the bridge from various angles, we lean against the railing of the pedestrian walkway. Hours fly by. The others left us long ago.

With a few squiggles, Cousin Pierre fixes my drawings. Papa will like them, but I have one more to make before daylight fades.

Standing on tiptoes, I look to where the river joins the sea, hoping for a glimpse of my subject. Swarms of people block my view.

"Ready to join the others?" Cousin Pierre asks.

"Almost. There's just one thing. Over there." I point across the water.

"Ah, of course. I should have guessed." He removes his watch from his vest pocket. "We've got time. Come on. Follow me."

We weave our way through the throngs. Finally, from our new spot I can see the project Papa and I have followed closely—the construction of the Liberty statue.

The sketches in the newspaper showed an enormous statue—several stories high—of a lady holding a torch. Squinting hard at little Bedloe's Island, I'm disappointed.

"Not much to see." Cousin Pierre shields his eyes from the setting sun.

"I thought at least I'd see the pedestal."

"Foundation first. They're digging down deep for that. Pretty soon they'll be pouring tons of concrete. You understand, don't you? The foundation's as important as the pedestal and the statue."

While Cousin Pierre describes the foundation, he draws and chats, barely lifting his eyes from the sketchpad. All afternoon I have been burning to tell him about my secret wish—to stand on this bridge. To see the cables and towers for myself. To see Miss Liberty. Would he understand? Would he laugh at me? Girls aren't supposed to wish for such things.

"I was here four years ago, Cousin Pierre. They haven't made much progress on Miss Liberty."

"Short on money. But it will happen. Someday."

A cool breeze rustles the paper on my sketchpad. Twilight forces us to stop drawing. Seagulls perched on a nearby tower glower down at us.

As I tuck my sketchbook away, Cousin Pierre studies the bridge's cables. The only sounds are peoples' voices and waves crashing against the base of the Brooklyn tower.

"I've had an absolutely wonderful day, sir. I've dreamed of being here for so long. It's even more wonderful than I imagined."

"I enjoyed your company, Miss Morgan. Not everyone shares your enthusiasm for this structure." He shakes his head, eyes wide. "The first all-steel bridge in the world. Even the wires are steel."

"I know."

"And they're using steel for the skeleton that will hold up Miss Liberty's copper skin."

"Papa says steel is the metal of the future. Which is funny because he just helped open the biggest iron foundry in Oakland."

"We'll always need iron. Couldn't make steel without it. One of its main ingredients. But steel's a lot lighter and stronger than iron. Great for skyscrapers."

"Skyscrapers?"

Is he teasing me? Cousin Pierre sees my puzzled look.

"Is this a new word for you?"

"Maybe," I admit.

"The word 'skyscraper' has lots of meanings," he explains. "A high-flying baseball, a tall man, but I mean it in the architectural sense, a building of incredible height."

I should have known. My face burns. He goes on. "A skyscraper is an extremely tall building, so tall it looks as if it . . . "

" . . . scrapes the sky?"

"Precisely! There's one going up in Chicago, ten stories high. Can you imagine? I want to build one in New York, with steel. Stronger than iron. Perfect for skyscrapers."

"Do what, dear?" Cousin Lucy hooks her arm into her husband's. Suddenly, my family crowds around us.

"Oh, something that wouldn't interest you. Isn't that right, Miss Morgan?" Cousin Pierre says, winking.

Emma, her voice quivering, says, "Cousin Pierre, I heard a scary story about the bridge."

"Did you?"

"About the bridge falling down," Avery pipes up. "I don't want that to happen. Not when we're on it." He stands so close to Mama he steps on Cousin Pierre's shoe.

Mama pulls Avery away. "Goodness, boy. Do hush up. How can you think such awful things?"

Perhaps my friend Mary was right to worry about the bridge falling down, after all.

Cousin Pierre frowns. "I'm sorry to tell you, Eliza, but there are a plenty of folks with nothing better to do than worry about such things."

Avery persists. "Isn't that what happened? That some people thought the bridge would fall?"

"Yes, young man. A few weeks back, just after the opening. All because one foolish man shouted, 'The bridge is falling!'"

"Why would anyone do such a thing?" Mama clutches Avery close.

"It's not clear. People ran. Some were trampled. It was terrible." He looked at our shocked faces. "But let me hasten to add that this bridge is the strongest in the world—much stronger than needed. You don't have to worry, Avery. Just ask your sister."

I try to explain to Emma and Avery how the cables work, but Avery is thinking about other things. "Please, Dudu. I want to know how the bridge made Mr. Roebling sick," he says.

"The bridge didn't make him sick, Avery. But building it did. Come on, I'll show you."

They follow me to a spot next to the Brooklyn tower. "Mr. Roebling didn't have scarlet fever. It was caisson disease," I explain. "Lots of bridge workers got it."

Avery squeezes next to me, clutching my hand.

"The caissons are giant steel boxes, bigger than two or three houses, and they're deep down in the water, under the towers."

"Where, Dudu? Show me."

"Down there," I say, pointing through a narrow opening to the water below. Emma and Avery look over the railing on their tiptoes.

"I don't see anything," shouts Avery. "Where are they?"

"They're underwater so we can't see them. But they're holding up those towers rising out of the water."

"I don't see what this has to do with Mr. Roebling getting sick." Emma says, staring through the opening to the water.

"I told you those caissons were deep, right? Going up and down those long ladders to get in and out was complicated. The men had to take their time."

"Why?" they ask together.

"Go too fast and you can get sick."

"Is that what happened to Mr. Roebling? He went up the ladder too fast?" Emma asks.

"Exactly. And that was that. He got caisson disease. Some men died. Mr. Roebling didn't die, but he couldn't walk anymore. He never left his bedroom. Now, look over there," I say, pointing to an apartment building along the edge of the river. "That's where he and his wife lived."

"But how could he build the bridge if he was in bed?" Emma asks.

I could have hugged her. In my opinion, the answer is the biggest miracle about this bridge.

"He couldn't have done it without Mrs. Roebling. Every day, Mr. Roebling checked the bridge's progress with his telescope. He could look right through his bedroom window. But every day, his wife did the real work."

"His wife?" Avery's eyes open wide. "Don't be silly, Dudu. Women don't work."

I did not argue with Avery, but secretly, I very much admire Mrs. Roebling. She was much more than a helper. Every day she talked with the workmen, explaining what Mr. Roebling wanted done.

Overhearing Cousin Pierre talking to Mama about me, I cannot help listening.

"Your daughter Julia reminds me of someone."

"And who would that be?" Mama asks.

"Emily Roebling, the Chief Engineer's wife. She was quick with numbers. She understood Roebling's ideas and the mathematics behind them."

Mama sniffs. "Odd behavior for a lady. Indeed, Julia is good with numbers, but she also knows her place."

Cousin Pierre's comments about my mathematical abilities lift my spirits. Mama's words send me crashing down to earth. He brings up a different subject. "Did we tell you about the big opening day party at the Roebling's place? Lucy and I were invited."

I inch closer. I read about the about the celebration, but my cousins were actually there.

Mama hooks her arm into Cousin Lucy's. "We heard President Grant attended. Did you see him?"

"Unfortunately, he'd already left."

"But we caught a glimpse of the rooster," adds Cousin Pierre.

Cousin Lucy laughs. "Indeed, we did!"

Avery stops throwing pebbles onto the road below. "What rooster?"

Cousin Lucy explains. "Poor Mr. Roebling was far too sick for the honorary first carriage ride over the bridge. So, Mrs. Roebling took his place. She rode the whole way with a rooster on her lap."

Emma laughs. "A rooster?"

"Yes, dear. A rooster, the symbol of victory, and believe me, finishing this bridge after so many years was a great victory."

I lean over the railing to watch an open carriage glide by, imagining Emily Roebling on her proud ride, a rooster on her lap.

At the moment when daylight dissolves into night, the electrified lamps lining the pedestrian walkway blink on. A collective "oh" is heard from everyone on the bridge.

New York City installed its first electrified streetlights a few months ago. Now they illuminate the greatest engineering feat in the world.

On our walk back to Remsen Street, my feet barely touch the cobblestones. My mind is filled with this amazing achievement—a bridge, breathtakingly beautiful and supremely strong. Clutching my precious sketchbook, I want to make this glorious feeling last. But then I remember Mama's disapproval of clever Mrs. Roebling. I suspect Mama and I would never agree about who is the real hero of the Brooklyn Bridge.

Chapter 4

HOME AGAIN

As we near Oakland, Avery and Emma scamper onto the train's maroon seat cushions, pressing their noses against the window. I'm right behind them. We are surrounded by water as the train rolls along the top of the longest pier in the world. Oh, how it dazzles—this Oakland Mole, stretching two long miles into the bay. A San Francisco ferry drifts so close I can count the passengers on its deck.

Despite his bad news, Papa smiles as he watches us depart the train. For the past several days, I imagined what was waiting for us in Oakland—a brand new house. Unfortunately, a leaking water pipe that damaged floors and walls will delay our moving in. In the meantime we must crowd into our too-small old house.

"Don't worry," Papa reassures us as we pile into the hired two-horse wagonette, big enough to hold the six of us and all our trunks. "We'll put Grandmother in the girls' room until the move. It is only for a few weeks."

Emma pouts, but I'm delighted. Tucked away in the attic, I can read for hours without Mama knowing.

We are home for a few minutes when I hear my friend Mary's special knock on the front door. Although I've been gone for only two months, she looks taller and tanner, her blond hair lightened by the summer sun. I doubt whether I've changed at all. I can still wear clothes from two years ago, and my hair is still boring black.

One look at her old dress and beat-up boots tells me exactly what she is planning.

"I'm glad you're back, Julia. I want to hear everything, so hurry up. Father wants me home by two," she says, green eyes shining.

"This way," I say, pointing down Fourteenth Street. "Best fences."

Most Oakland houses are surrounded by low-set iron or picket fences that connect one lot to the other. Mary and I prefer the pickets. The narrow wood crossbeams nailed along their backside become our raised sidewalk, a perfect fit for our small feet.

After a few blocks, we hop off. We have arrived at our special tree, a giant Monterey pine. A low-hanging limb makes an easy first step. The rest of the way up is like climbing a ladder.

Sitting on our favorite branch high above the ground we hear the clip-clop of horses' hooves as they pull wagons and carriages along the earthen-packed street below.

Mary squints into the distance. "My house looks so tiny from up here. Can you see yours?"

Leaning left, I easily spot our new home. Standing alone on the corner of Brush and Fourteenth, it looks ready for my family's invasion.

"The church is pretty from here, isn't it?" Mary says, legs swinging. Her house and the church where her father, Reverend McLean, is the popular minister, sit side-by-side like old friends.

Plucking off a pinecone, she drops it. Silently I tick off the seconds while we watch it fall. As usual, it takes three to land.

After dropping another, she turns toward me. "So how was it, Julia? Did you see your bridge?"

"I did!"

"And?"

"It was wonderful. And no, Mary, it didn't fall down. In fact, I don't think it ever will. Not the way it's built. Those towers. I've told you about them. Huge. Massive. Two of them. Tallest structures in the entire world. Made of steel, of course."

"You've gone on about that bridge ever since we met."

Usually, I'm the one who listens to Mary's stories, but not today. Sitting on the pine tree's branch, I tell her about the bridge, its beauty and its strength. I make her laugh with witty comments about my silly brothers. I explain how hard this move is for my grandmother.

Mary plucks a few stray pine needles from her wool stockings. "You were gone a long time. I'm glad you're back," she says.

"Yep, just in time for school."

Mary drops another pinecone. "Someday I'm going to see your bridge, Julia. But for now, let's find some more fences."

* * *

Months later, Emma and I are still sleeping in the attic. Mama doesn't want to move until everything is just right. When moving day finally arrives, my things are packed, and the attic is empty. While Mama and our cook, Bridget, are busy giving the movers directions, Papa and I leave for the new house. I tamp down the desire to run all the way to 754 Fourteenth Street.

The outside of our house is decorated with more gables, turrets, and cutout wood shapes than most. Racing up the front steps, my fingers brush the elegant carved-wood railing. When Papa turns the key in the lock, the wide front door swings open. We stand in the doorway, savoring the moment.

"Dudu, let in some light before the others arrive."

My boots tap-tap on the colorful tile entryway, echoing throughout the giant empty space. Racing from room to room, I pull open the drapes, inhaling the odors of fresh paint, wood varnish, and new rugs. There is an indescribable magic in this big, empty space, soon to be filled with our furniture and our lives.

When Mama's friends make their first calls, they marvel over everything, from the gas stove to the luxury of indoor plumbing. Papa usually guides his friends to his study then out back to the boys' gymnasium equipment set up in the carriage house.

Mary is wide-eyed during her first visit, and at first chance she whispers, "Julia, your mother has turned into an absolute gigglemug."

She's right. Mama has not stopped smiling for days.

Mary is uncharacteristically quiet until we arrive at the kitchen. "Oh my!" she exclaims so many times I lose count.

"It's only an oven," I say.

"But so new, and shiny. And gas! Mother hates her coal stove—the fumes and dirt. Everything's so beautiful here."

She follows me to the carriage house. Luckily, we have the place to ourselves. In the beginning, the boys were dead set against my using the gymnastic equipment. Parm even blocked my way, but I fixed that. I stared into his eyes, then uttered a single word—"MOVE." After a slight hesitation, he stepped aside. The boys have not interfered with me since.

Mary and I turn our long skirts into pantaloons by pulling the back hems between our legs then tucking them into our front waistbands. With our legs free, we climb onto the parallel bars, do a few tricks, then sit on a single bar, side-by-side.

"Your new house is so big," Mary says.

"Big houses do have their problems," I say, still smarting from my latest dust up with Parmelee.

"Like what?"

"In our old house, my parents knew everything we did. But here Parm has discovered new ways to torment me without them knowing."

"Like what?"

"He's hiding my letters from Cousin Pierre. He knows how I wait for them. The first letter he snatched was my fault. I accidently left it lying out. I got it back, but at a cost—my blue aggie."

"Not your aggie. My favorite marble."

"Oh, but it was worth it."

I do not tell Mary about the thrilling details of the letter, like how my bridge survived several violent winter storms. Mary's eyelids tend to droop when I go on like that.

When Cousin Pierre and I stood on the Brooklyn Bridge together, he assured me that the extra cables Roebling added would stand up to anything. Powerful hurricane winds, waves, and flying objects—nothing could harm the bridge. On the other hand, the Liberty statue worries me. Ninety feet high, standing alone, unprotected in the New York harbor, she may be no match for Mother Nature. Cousin Pierre's letters keep me up to date.

* * *

Weeks later, Parm's letter-snatching turns bolder, but his smirk gives him away.

"Okay, Parm. Hand it over."

"Hand what over?"

"You know what."

He laughs. "Okay. You can have it if you give me . . . "

I steel myself for another outrageous demand. Fortunately, he wants two of my luckiest glass hopscotch markers. It's worth the price since I no longer play hopscotch. Over the next several weeks, Parm is so wrapped up with his friends that he forgets to steal my letters. I'm hopeful that problems with my annoying brother are over.

Chapter 5

A NATION MOURNS

That fall I start at Irving Grammar School, located inside Oakland High School. Even though we must use the back door, I do catch occasional glimpses of the high schoolers.

I love this demanding new world, even all the assignments. If I get overwhelmed, an hour or two practicing my violin puts me right. So does drawing with my pastels.

By the second year at Irving, other kids are asking me for help, and President Ulysses S. Grant dies. The *Oakland Tribune* decorates its front page with a black border. My teacher, Miss Peterson, speaks somberly about his passing. "The nation is mourning the loss of a great man. Who remembers when he came to Oakland?"

A lone hand shoots up.

"Mary?"

"Yes, ma'am. I think I was about seven. My father was on the official Welcoming Committee. I got to sit in the review stands."

Mary remembers correctly. That's when we first met, as new pupils at Lafayette Primary School.

"Now class, President Grant's burial will be in New York on August 8. Here in Oakland, on the same day, hour, and minute of his burial, we too shall observe his passing. This promises to be a memorable day, and all of you will take part."

That night I tell Mama the details. "We'll need black sashes, all four of us. White dresses for girls. White shirts for boys."

Emma, face flushed, interrupts. "There'll be thousands of us, Mama, all marching. And bands, and horses, and flowers, lots of flowers."

Papa puts down his paper. "That was today's topic at the Republican Club. We will show San Francisco how this should be done. That city across the bay had no plans until they caught wind of ours."

I saved the most important bit for last. "Principal McChesney says he needs help from all the mothers."

Mama sighs. Four of us Morgan kids are in three different schools—Emma and Avery at my old school, me at Irving, and Parm now in Oakland High. Mama will be busier than ever.

Still, she doesn't dilly-dally. That evening she sends invitations to the neighborhood women. For several days they gather at our house, sewing hundreds of black and white fabric rosettes for each child's shirt or blouse and a banner for us to march behind. Our big home is chaotic, every room downstairs filled with fabric, activity, and bottomless pots of hot tea.

While I'm amused by the preparations, I'm annoyed by how the fuss, especially the rehearsal at Harrison Park, interferes with our schoolwork. We are made to sit and stand countless times, all three thousand of us. Up and down, up and down, until we do it together.

I spend the time watching the workmen construct an elaborate stage for the three hundred speakers and dignitaries. They struggle to attach three heavy arches to the back of the stage. When we finally march back to school, I glance over my shoulder in time to see the arches wobble when a workman brushes against one. More alarming is how the arches lean the tiniest bit toward the speaker's podium.

On the morning of the ceremony the city echoes with church bells, cannons, and fire station gongs. Black buntings drape balconies, doorways, and banisters. Before Mary and I line up with the others, we inspect the blue-and-gold silk banner our mothers made, black ribbons hanging from either end.

Mary reads aloud. "*We welcomed him living, September 25, 1879. We mourn him dead, August 8, 1885.*"

"Eloquent, Mary, don't you think?"

"Indeed."

Miss Peterson rests her hand on Mary's shoulder. "Miss McLean. In line please. Miss Morgan, this includes you."

Drum corps and marching bands join our parade to the park.

Like everyone else, I wave my little American flag with one hand and clutch a bouquet of flowers in the other. At Harrison Park, I follow the line of kids past a giant wire container with an oversized picture of President Grant on top. We toss our bouquet of red, white, and blue posies inside as we pass. During the ceremony, I keep an eye on those shaky arches now draped with heavy black fabric decorated with black-and-white rosettes and hanging green vines.

After tucking my rosette into my drawer that night, I spot the protractor Papa gave me. Shaped like a half-circle, it helps me draw perfect right angles. As I practice, I wonder why the workmen had not done a better job of checking the accuracy of their angles. The dignitaries survived unscathed, but now I have right angles on my mind. I create several sketches of how I would have attached the arches to the stage, checking angles with my protractor.

Aware that Cousin Pierre may be interested in Oakland's ceremonies, I write him the details. After Christmas, his letter arrives with good news about Miss Liberty. The pieces of the statue are on the boat from Paris to New York. I have read each of his letters so often, they begin tearing along the fold. I hide them in an old cookie tin under my bed. Each time I read one over, I imagine myself leaning against the railing of the Brooklyn Bridge, next to Cousin Pierre.

As June nears, I wait anxiously for his letter about the statue's arrival. When I finally tear it open, I'm disappointed with his news.

June 25, 1885

Dear Julia,
The statue arrived in New York Harbor last week. There was a huge gathering of ships to escort the Isère and its precious cargo through the narrows and into the harbor. I watched from the deck of my

friend's yacht. We were surrounded by so many boats it was like being in the middle of a gigantic maritime picnic. Later, I learned that members of the welcome committee had trouble getting from their boat onto the larger, higher Isère. A few of the braver dignitaries walked up to the ship on a shaky gangplank, and once aboard, jumped down into the hold where all the crates were stored. There are reports they glimpsed a curl of the lady's hair, and a bit of her nose.

Unfortunately, there is bad news. The pedestal is not finished. This means that all those crates with those thousands of pieces are to be stored away. I'll let you know what happens.

Chapter 6

TOO MANY QUESTIONS

That fall, Sam boasts to everyone that he finally started Lafayette Primary School. Every day he comes home with a story about another new friend. If he doesn't know someone, he promptly introduces himself.

From when he was a baby, he chose me for comforting, nighttime tuck-ins, and the like. It was always "Dudu do it," or "Dudu make it better." These days he shows me a painful splinter. He doesn't cry when I clean his cuts. I'm the one to put the icepack on his bumps and bruises.

One day at school while playing chase with a new pal, he takes a bad fall. He doesn't let anyone peek at his injury, not even me. By bedtime, our cheerful, happy Sam is a silent, cross stranger.

At tuck-in, I ask him once more if he'll show me his elbow. Finally, he nods. As I feared, the wound is red and tender. "You can wash it," he says, eyes brimming before I even begin.

"I'll be careful, Sam. Promise." Gently, I dab his elbow. "Did you fall down?"

"Uh huh."

He doesn't cry, but I can see pebbles stuck deep in the wound. The next morning, his elbow is swollen to twice its size. Mama sends for Dr. Wilcox.

Usually brave, when Sam hears the doctor's knock at the front door, he crumbles, his lower lip quivering. I take his small hand in mine. When the doctor walks into the parlor, Sam squeezes my hand so hard it hurts.

Dr. Wilcox inspects the elbow. "You say this happened yesterday, Mrs. Morgan?"

Mama nods. "Yes, Doctor."

He looks at the injury again. "Hmmm."

As he turns the arm for a better look, Sam whimpers.

"Good you called, Mrs. Morgan. This kind of wound can get nasty alarmingly fast."

"I know," Mama responds, her usually pink cheeks now sheet white. To Sam she says, "Do what Dr. Wilcox tells you. I'll be back." Briskly, she leaves the room.

Dr. Wilcox removes his black waistcoat, rolls up his sleeves, then opens his black bag. Sam squeezes my hand harder.

"Now, Sam, I need you to be brave," the doctor says, peering over the rim of his glasses. "This is going to hurt."

"May I help, sir?" I ask, hoping to help calm Sam, or at least distract him from what is coming. I'm also eager to watch.

"Could be useful, Miss Morgan, if you think you're up to it."

"I am," I say, sounding more confident than I feel.

As long as the doctor doesn't follow the instructions in Mama's *Practical Housekeeping* book, I should be fine. I have memorized the entire chapter on household accidents. It's grim but riveting: *The wound should be cut open to provide a way of escape for the blood. A piece of linen wet with laudanum should then be inserted in the wound. Then wrap the wound with a strip of linen.*

While Dr. Wilcox pulls various instruments from his black bag, I sit close to Sam. Beads of sweat dot his forehead. His hand feels clammy and cold. While we wait, Bridget appears with a bowl of warm water and a white cloth already cut into strips.

A bar of soap is the last item Dr. Wilcox takes from his bag. Holding it up, he looks at me. "My best cure for these kinds of injuries, Miss Morgan. Familiar with it?"

"Soap, sir. But I'm guessing it's not ordinary soap."

"Indeed not. It's carbolic soap." He looks at Sam. "Young man, time to wash that elbow of yours. Now I'm not going to sugarcoat this. It's going to sting, a lot. But imagine you're a soldier in the Civil War. Those were mighty brave men, weren't they?"

Sam nods.

"Did the Civil War doctors use this soap?" I ask.

"They sure did."

The carbolic soap must hurt because by the time Dr. Wilcox finishes, the entire household crowds into the parlor, alarmed by Sam's screams.

"Finished," Dr. Wilcox says at last, tying a linen strip around Sam's angry red elbow.

With hair plastered to his damp forehead, Sam manages a weak smile. Holding his hand, I wonder if the doctor might answer some questions. "Dr. Wilcox . . . "

"Yes, Miss Morgan," he says, putting his tweezer back into his medical bag.

"How does the carbolic soap work?"

Before he answers, I ask another. "Why didn't you open up the wound and let the bad blood out?" And another. "How often should we change the linen wrap?"

I have more but these will have to do. Bridget is already helping Dr. Wilcox with his jacket. Time is short.

"Excellent questions. Let's see. Well, for starters, we're not sure how carbolic soap works, but it's nothing like those Ivory soap bars."

Ivory soap is a family favorite. Because the bars float, Sam likes to pretend they are ships. When he was younger, we would find him in the bathtub with a whole fleet of bars bobbing around.

"And of course, with the carbolic soap I didn't have to open his elbow."

"And the wrap?"

"Change it daily. Tie it up this way, and wash the soiled linen strips well, then hang them in the sun to dry. Sunlight dries the bandages faster, keeps them cleaner."

While Dr. Wilcox answers my questions, I think of those long months in Brooklyn when I was sick with scarlet fever. I can picture Dr. Johnson, who cared for us. I remember his warm hands and his soothing voice calming my fears. I remember looking into his eyes. I was only six, but he comforted me at a scary time.

As the doctor heads to the front door, Mama returns. "Lands' sake, Dudu. Leave the good doctor alone," she scolds. "I do apologize," she says to Dr. Wilcox. "Our Julia is inclined to ask too many questions." Opening the front door she adds, "Frankly doctor, I have yet to discover a subject that doesn't interest her."

* * *

For the remainder of the year, Sam's scrapes and bruises are easier to fix. By spring, I have another urgent matter. My church's annual musical fete is fast approaching. Even though Emma and I play every year, this is Avery's first time. My teacher, Miss De Pisa, chose a demanding piece for me, but I love the intricate bowing.

Despite practicing daily, a few passages sorely test me. Fortunately, I have studied violin long enough to know that persistence pays. *Have patience. Do it again. And again. And once more.* Soon there is the satisfaction of flawless execution.

By the night of the fete, I'm ready. As the eldest and only eighth grade musician, I play last, which gives me time to study the audience. Papa and Mama sit in the front row with Grandmother and Sam between them. Sam's hair is neatly oiled and parted. Parm sits in the back with friends.

When it is my turn, the pianist, Mr. Taylor, signals he is ready. While I tune my violin, the room quiets, except for the occasional cough, rustle of skirts, or flutter of ladies' fans. As soon as I lift my bow, those sounds dim. My violin allows me to express myself without words. With the *crescendo*, I use firm bow strokes that make the music louder. With the *adagio*, I slow the bowing and the music softens. But my favorite is *molto vivace*, when the melody is light and lively, yet strong, determined, sure-footed.

As the last note fades, enthusiastic applause jolts me back into the real world. Violin by my side, I curtsy, absorbing the audience's smiling faces. I'm further surprised at the reception afterwards. Strangers approach me.

"You were brilliant!"

"Such an accomplished player for one so young."

"Wonderful bowing."

And then I hear another comment. "You would make a wonderful music teacher."

For an instant, I imagine myself as a music teacher. I do love music. It unlocks something precious deep within me. But teaching music is so different from making music. And then there is medicine, which interests me, but interest alone is not enough.

As I tuck my violin into its case, I realize Mama is right. I have several interests. Medicine, music. But that day when I stood on the Brooklyn Bridge with Cousin Pierre, sketchbook in hand, something magical happened. A yearning, a kind of hunger formed deep within me, a feeling I cannot put into words, not yet. One thing is clear, however. I must find a way to keep that feeling alive.

Chapter 7

THE INVISIBLE LINE

T hanks to geomètry, my final year at Irving Grammar
School zips by. My teacher says I have a knack for
drawing all those lines and angles. At the last assembly,
I am asked to play my violin. Miss De Pisa advises Vivaldi's
Concerto in A Minor, the first movement which is more
challenging than what I played at last spring's musical fete.
When I play this piece, I'm full of hope and joy, and why
not? Oakland High School awaits me.

First, however, there is the matter of the final school
exam. As a top student, I'm not worried, but a test is a test.

By the time Mary and I walk into the examination
hall, most seats are taken by other ninth graders from
Oakland's grammar schools.

The teacher in charge rings a bell on his desk. "You
may begin."

During the next three hours the hall is quiet, except for
the scratching of pencils on paper, an occasional cough,
or the shuffling of feet.

"Time! Hands on the desk."

I inspect my pencil—no teeth marks, a good sign.

"Scores will be posted on Monday. If you pass, you need not attend the last week of school."

Mary, two rows ahead of me, turns around to smile. Undoubtedly, she has a plan figured out for our free week.

* * *

When we arrive at Mary's house later that day, I lower my voice to a whisper. "Now remember, not a word to your mother."

Mary rests the back of her hand against her forehead. "A tragedy. Our last roller-skate."

"It may be our last, but it'll be our best ever."

"I'll say. See you soon."

Curiously, last week our mothers issued the identical warning on the exact same day. "No more roller-skating."

"But Mama, you can't mean it?" I wailed.

"I do. It's time you act your age."

Lately, Mama has a lot to say about what young ladies can and cannot do. She rarely misses an opportunity to tell me when I cross her invisible line—a line I would rather erase.

The sidewalk in front of my house is crowded with skaters, Emma among them. I smile until I remember this is my last skate. Then I console myself. This might be the last skate Mama *knows* about.

As I open the front door, the smell of fresh-baked bread fills the cool, dark interior of my home. Light streams through the stained-glass window at the top of the staircase, dotting the floor with a rainbow of color.

Hanging my coat and hat on the hallway rack, I glance at my reflection in its small mirror. Mama finally gave in to my pleas. Gone are my shoulder length curls and bangs. These days I pull my hair back into a bun at the nape of my neck.

I head for the kitchen and Bridget's lemon dream cookies. Parm must be away, or the cookie plate would be empty by now. Bridget looks up from her mixing bowl. "Miss Julia, I'm glad you're home. Your grandmother's been asking for you."

"I'll go right away, Bridget. And thanks for saving these from my hungry brother."

Grandmother and I have a special ritual. It started when she arrived in Oakland. We saw how she grew restless in those hours before dinner. Mama asked me to read to her. I didn't mind. It gave us something to do together. Now, for a few minutes each day, I'm invited into Grandmother's private parlor to read her favorite Bible stories aloud. Increasingly, our time together becomes the highlight of her day, or so Mama says.

"Before you start, Dudu, please bring me today's newspaper. I declare. How I miss my *Daily Eagle*. This Oakland paper is filled with stories about people I don't know."

By the time I'm back, Grandmother's eyes are already closed, her rocker still. I place the newspaper on the table beside her before tiptoeing out.

Shouts from the garden shatter the calm.

"It's my turn. That's not fair."

"Oh, come on, Sam. You're too little."

"Please, Avery. Please."

Every day it's the same—the boys squabbling over the gymnasium equipment. Parm, with one more year of high school, is rarely around, which is unfortunate. He knows how to keep the younger boys in line. Now, Avery and Sam, left to their own devices, discover new and more dangerous challenges.

Of course, none are as good as my favorite but soon-to-be-forbidden trick. Like roller-skating, my gymnastic days are also numbered. Mama will not listen to reason. "It's time, Dudu. Maybe I shouldn't have permitted it in the first place. Too much exercise is not healthy for girls, nor is it proper."

Grandmother is on Mother's side, and of course Papa agrees with Mama on everything. Once again I'm outnumbered.

I slip on my bloomers hanging behind the carriage house door. Sam and Avery stop squabbling when I walk in. Despite my skirt, petticoats, and tight-fitting blouse, I pull myself up onto the double bars and manage a somer-sault with the bars supporting my shoulders. After a brief pause, I repeat the trick. Two in a row! A first! After a quick dismount, I dust off my hands, smooth my skirt, and give the boys a smart salute. Despite my smile, I'm already mourning the end of my gymnastic career.

Mary knocks promptly at three. We sit on the front steps, inspecting our roller skates.

"Golly. Look at this. A chipped wheel," I complain.

"I guess our good old skates are just that—old," Mary groans. "I've got a chunk out of mine, too. Wooden wheels do that. Mother will never let me buy a new pair."

"I should have filed mine down earlier," I say, resting my boot on the skate's wooden platform—still a perfect fit.

"I'll buckle yours if you do mine," Mary offers.

Expertly, she tightens the leather straps, one around my ankle, and the other across my toes.

Mary grumbles while I do her straps, "I still think Mother's wrong. Skating *is* ladylike. It's like dancing."

"My mother agrees with your mother."

Mary sighs. "Mothers."

"Mothers," I echo.

Lately, I have less patience for Mama's insistence that I do everything her way. I know she wants what is best for me, but she makes me feel like a piece of a puzzle that doesn't fit anywhere.

To make matters worse, little by little, everything I love is taken away. "Not good for you." "Not proper." "You're getting older." And one I detest the most, "What will the young men think?"

Two little boys zipping by us on wobbly skates interrupt my dark thoughts.

"Ah, the innocence of childhood," Mary says, hands pressed to her heart.

Standing, I grab her hand. "Come on. Let's make the most of our fleeting days of childhood."

Linking arms, we skate around the entire block. I used to fall all the time on the bumpy wooden sidewalks. The newly poured cement changes this. Now when I skate, nothing can stop me. I'm strong, fast, and free, taking secret delight in skating circles around the boys, who stumble like clumsy penguins. After several more flawless runs around the block, Mary's ready to quit.

"I'm starved," she admits.

"Still searching for a cook?"

She nods.

Unbuckling our skates, I think I hear her stomach rumbling.

"Want to stay for dinner? Bridget's making pot roast. There'll be plenty."

"Pot roast! Oh, yes, please!"

Mama is surprisingly cheerful when I ask if Mary can stay. "Good. There's something important we must discuss."

Something important? Now my stomach does a little dance. Nothing good ever happens when Mama uses those words.

Chapter 8

FROM LITTLE ACORNS

Mama waits for us to finish eating before interrogating Mary. "What are your summer plans, dear?"

"Camping, ma'am. My father loves it. Much more than Mother, I'm afraid."

Mary entertains us with a story of their last trip, ruined by an unwelcome thunderstorm flooding their site. When she finishes, Mama clears her throat, eyeing Papa. He taps his water glass with a spoon.

"Attention, everyone. Mother would like a word, and it involves all of you."

Mama eyes me and Mary. "Congratulations, girls, on completing your high school qualifying examination. I have no doubt you will both be admitted."

I glance at Mary, rosy faced from the attention.

Parm interrupts. "Excuse me, Mama." He pushes back his chair. "I'd like to add a word here—something that must be said."

I hold my breath.

"As an illustrious member of the Oakland High School Graduating Class of 1888, I'd like to welcome you both to my beloved school. However, I do have a small request." Frowning, he stares at us. The room is silent. Finally, he speaks. "Do not embarrass me!"

I cannot tell if the laughter is because of his joke or because everyone is relieved that he didn't say something awful. Now I stand.

"Dear brother. The exact opposite can also be said. Don't *you* embarrass us!"

When the laughter stops, Mama goes on.

"In honor of the completion of your grammar school education, your father and I have decided to host an afternoon tea. Mary, you and your parents must join us. It will be a small affair—a few of your school friends and a few of ours."

I'm surprised. My parents rarely praise any of us in public. I suspect that this party is an excuse for Mama to impress her friends with our newly planted garden.

The worst part of Mama's party idea is that I will be the center of attention. There will be comments about my clothes, my hair, my hat. People will look at me, judge me. How I detest this. And the truth of the matter is that when it comes to Mama's social events, there is no such thing as a "small affair."

A few days later, after the delivery boy sets off with the bundle of invitations, Mama schedules several appointments that naturally include Grandmother. The first is with Mrs. Neldam—the best seamstress in town. In a single afternoon, Mama checks off several items on her list, including ordering my dress for the party as well as my wardrobe for high school.

Mama is clear on this last item. "A few simple shirt-waists for my high school girl, Mrs. Neldam. High collars, a bit of lace at the wrists, and pearl buttons down the front. Colors—white, pale blue, and pale yellow. And two or three skirts to go with them. How does that sound, Dudu?"

"Very nice, Mama." I mean it. Simple is what I like.

"And two jackets, Mrs. Neldam, dark with matching trim."

Mrs. Neldam spreads out a dozen swatches of material. Mama picks two, both shades of brown. Two other swatches catch my eye, one dark teal green, and the other charcoal grey. Both would go well with my skirts. If I don't say something now, I will be stuck with dull brown jackets for the year.

"Mrs. Neldam," I say, holding up my choices. "Mama knows a lot more about such matters, but how do you like these?"

I avoid looking at Mama.

"Your daughter has a good eye for color, Mrs. Morgan. How proud you must be," says the clever Mrs. Neldam as she makes a note of my choices. "Now regarding your party dress . . . "

Here, things do not go as well. Mama insists on frills and ruffles, and of course, a modest bustle. Using all my persuasive powers, I convince her to choose a less fussy design of pale lavender silk. Neither my mother nor grandmother will budge on the corset I must wear under my dress. It squeezes my ribs so tightly I can scarcely breathe, but they are adamant.

The trip to the milliner's shop is exhausting and maddening. Mama picks all the wrong silk flowers for my hat—too many, and too loud. Whenever I suggest a different color, Mama says, "Pish posh, Dudu. I know what's best." Several times I wanted to jump up from the milliner's chair and run away. By the time we finish, the hat looks like a gaudy flower garden. I withhold my complaints. Mama's hat is twice the size of mine.

Things at home are hectic. Jack, our gardener, works hard trimming hedges, planting flowers, and spreading new gravel on the walkways. Bridget fills the pantry with sweets.

❋ ❋ ❋

On the day of the party, Emma helps tighten my corset. If she pulls any tighter, she will break my ribs. Standing before the full-length mirror, Mama secures my hat. Despite the profusion of flowers, it is not as showy as I had feared.

Once the guests arrive, I keep my distance from Mama. I know what she will say. "We're so proud of Julia. She did well on her exams," or "Julia is such a serious little bookworm." The worst of all, "Julia is so quiet lately we worry that she'll disappear."

Mary's mother, Mrs. McLean, corners me by the punch bowl where I help fill our guests' crystal cups.

"Such a nice party, Julia. Mary's been terribly excited about the whole affair." She pauses to sip her punch. "Now that you and Mary are off to high school, I imagine you'll be busier than ever."

"Yes, ma'am."

"Especially with the coming social season. Which reminds me. I must talk to your mother about dance lessons for you and Mary. Never too early to be ready for the debutante balls."

Mrs. McLean raises her parasol before making a beeline for Mama. Debutante balls. How I detest those two words. These days Mama sprinkles them into every conversation. She and Grandmother spend hours poring over newspaper stories about the latest coming-out parties, who attended, their dresses, and which band played. This is the social highlight of the year for Oakland's well-to-do families. Not surprisingly, Mama and I don't see eye-to-eye on the subject.

While I wait for Bridget to refill the punch bowl, I catch snatches of Mrs. McLean's conversation with Mama.

"Oh, yes, you're right. Emma is the beauty in the family," Mama agrees.

I don't hear Mrs. McLean's reply, but Mama's words are clear. "Yes, that's true. Julia has the brains."

Mama is right. Emma is certainly the beauty. But there's nothing wrong with being smart. It's my brain that's going to get me into college. Oh, yes, I'm going to college.

This is a new idea, dropping on me like those acorns falling from our oak tree. I pick up one our gardener missed, and tuck it away for safekeeping.

❋   ❋   ❋

A few days later, summer vacation starts with my family boarding the train to the seaside town of Santa Cruz. Mama waits until we nearly arrive before saying, "Dudu, I think it's time we expand your interests."

I'm on high alert, familiar with her tone.

"I have interests, Mama. My violin. The piano."

"Thank goodness for that. But when we return, you and Emma will start lessons at the Simmons Social Dancing Academy. Mr. Simmons prepares all the young people in Oakland for the season. Parmelee did well there, and so will you."

Hearing the finality in Mama's voice, I squelch my protest. Instead, I think about Parm's "interests," which are often the subject of his talks with Papa. My father has strong ideas about what Parm should do after he graduates from high school. Parm rejects them all, and I know why. My brother's interests center on one thing—spending nights with his rowdy friends.

As the train chugs south, Mama's comment about Emma's beauty and my brains echoes in my mind. Absentmindedly, I finger the small acorn I picked up at the garden party and have taken to keeping in my pocket. Rubbing its smooth shell, I have a single thought. *"Mighty oaks from little acorns grow." Yes, that will be me. While it is true I may be nothing more than a tiny acorn today, tomorrow is another story.*

I open my sketchbook, then set up my pastels. By the time we near Santa Cruz, my drawing is complete. A large, leafy oak shades a small house similar to ours. Next to the tree I draw a tiny acorn, its delicate roots reaching into the dark, rich soil. How does a tiny seed with such fragile roots grow strong enough to support a giant oak? As we pull into the depot, this image fills my head.

Part II
The Choice

Oakland High School

Chapter 9

"STRAIGHT LINES, MY GIRL"

When we return from Santa Cruz, Mama insists I accompany her on her daily social calls. "My friends want a glimpse of you, Dudu."

The worst part of these visits is how I must answer the ladies' predictable questions like, "When will you be coming out?" And, "What will you be studying in high school?"

I mumble something about how my coming out is still a few years off. When I tell them I will be in "The Scientific Track," all the ladies have the same reaction. Although they are expert at hiding their true feelings, I know disapproval when I see it—an eyebrow twitch, the slight flare of nostrils, or a hand tightening around a teacup handle.

Mrs. Bigelow especially excels at dispensing unwanted advice. "I didn't think girls studied those sorts of things," she says with a watery smile. "And besides, what does a lady need with science?"

Even though her words are meant for me, she looks at Mama. While this sentiment stings, it comes as no surprise. I hear it often. *Girls should apply themselves to singing, drawing, dancing, and learning a foreign language. Anything else is wasteful.*

Artfully, Mama changes the subject. "Did you know that young Mary McLean will study literature? She's quite well-read, you know."

Mrs. Bigelow sniffs. "Such a sensible girl. A far more suitable subject for a young lady."

While Mama never utters a word of reproach about my choice of studies, we have not discussed it. Those conversations are reserved for Papa. The two of us spend hours poring over the Oakland High School Register, the little booklet that describes the classes for all three years.

One night after flipping through the pamphlet, Papa reads aloud. "Mechanical Drawing. How to draw oblique, isometric, and orthographic projections of solids, including their sections, intersection, and developments."

Puffing his cigar, Papa sits back in his chair. "An interesting requirement for the Scientific Track, Dudu. Even though I never formally studied mechanical drawing, the subject has always fascinated me. You're going to need special tools for these classes, you know. In fact, I've been thinking that the two of us should go to San Francisco to buy yours."

❋ ❋ ❋

I have visited San Francisco with Papa in the past, but this is the first time it is just the two of us. As the ferry inches closer to the fog-shrouded terminal across the bay, I complete my quick survey of the newest buildings. There are several four or five stories high, some built with brick but most of wood.

On our walk to the store, Papa is more talkative than usual. "If I had gone to college, I'm sure I would have studied mechanical drawing," he admits.

I hurry to keep up. "I liked drawing in grammar school," I say, out of breath.

"And you're good, Dudu. But mechanical drawing isn't the same thing. You'll see. The tools we buy today will become your best friends. It's all about angles, lines, and precise measurements."

I think about the protractor in my drawer at home, the one from Papa, the one I use for drawing angles in geometry. I expect these new tools to be even more fun.

The salesman sets out several sets of drafting tools on the counter's glass top. We inspect each one. Finally, he pushes a plain pine box with brass fittings toward us. "This set is well priced for a new student."

Snapping open the box, Papa lifts out the largest tool. "Feel the weight of this compass, Dudu," he says, handing me the instrument with two hands. "Try it out."

Carefully, I set the compass up on its two long, slender legs, my fingers grasping the top.

"Well balanced," Papa says, approvingly. "Close it up and hold it in your hand."

Slim as a long, narrow pen, it feels both substantial and delicate.

Lastly, we purchase the T square. It is the length of a baseball bat and opens into the shape of a letter T. "Nothing could be more useful. Mark my words, Dudu. This one has the right weight and is perfectly crafted. Straight lines, my girl. Essential. You'll see." Papa carries it home under his arm.

* * *

Back home, Mary is pacing on the front porch. I race up the steps, two at a time.

"What is it, Mary?"

"Guess what's happening at my house. Go ahead. Guess."

"I can't." Mary knows I detest such games, but that never stops her.

"I'll give you a clue. We have a guest."

"You always have guests."

It's true. The McLeans have frequent visitors, many staying for days, even weeks. Mostly they're church missionaries touring America, giving talks about the people they help. Still, I have never seen Mary so excited.

"Come on, Mary. Tell me."

"His name is George Tuttle. He's got the darkest eyes and longest eyelashes I've ever seen on a boy. And here's the best part. He's going to Oakland High with us!"

Cheeks ablaze, Mary babbles on. "His parents are missionaries in Hawaii. They've sent him here to finish his education, and he'll be living in *our* house. He has one more year of high school, and then he's off to some eastern college. Isn't this thrilling?"

I want to tell her how a boy in the house changes everything. My own three brothers are proof. Being an only child, she has no idea.

"He's very nice, very polite. He'll be a senior in the Literary Track. I'm supposed to show him around Oakland before school starts."

"And you're just the person, Mary."

"What do you mean, 'you'? This is a two-person job. Mother agrees."

"Mary! How could you?"

"Oh, Julia, don't be a spoilsport. It'll be fun. I have four tickets to the circus, free as usual."

We go every year when the Sells Brothers Circus is in town. The roustabouts set up their tent on the empty lot next door to the McLean's. Circus workers fill bucket after bucket of fresh water for their thirsty animals. In exchange for unlimited use of their water faucet, the circus gives the McLeans four free tickets.

Still, I'm certain Mary isn't telling me everything.

Resting her hands on my shoulders, she stares at me. "We need another boy to go with us, Julia. Someone who'll make him feel welcome. Someone his age."

"Mary, please. I told you I'm not going."

"Oh, come on, Julia. Don't you think it's important that we extend hospitality to the boy, a stranger in a strange land?"

"And which boy are you thinking about?"

"Why Parmelee, of course."

How shrewd of Mary. If Parmelee is our escort to the circus, Mama will agree to my going. The question is will he be polite or an obnoxious show-off?

*   *   *

Mary turns out to be right about George. He's tall, handsome, polite, and laughs heartily in all the right places. He even buys each of us a bag of fresh roasted peanuts. Sitting between Parm and George, holding the warm bag of peanuts; I'm glad I came. There are those familiar smells like fresh sawdust on the floor, the animals, and of course, the peanuts. But there is a new smell—Parm's shaving soap. Glancing at his face, I spot the faint but distinct outline of a moustache on his upper lip. My silly, vain brother.

"Best circus ever," Mary says afterwards as we head to my house for a glass of Bridget's lemonade.

"First circus ever," George confides.

"Glad we could oblige, old man," Parm says, whacking George on the back, harder than needed.

"I couldn't get enough of those hippopotamuses," Mary exclaims. "Or should I say hippopotami?"

"You've been studying your Latin, and school hasn't even started," teases Parm. "You're a regular eager beaver."

"Good for you," George says, rewarding Mary with a smile. "Actually, I'm looking forward to school. I know it's only a year, but I could use some fun. I've had nothing but tutors. So, Parmelee, tell me. What do I need to know about the place?"

"Here's the most important thing you need to know, old man. Most of the girls are the jammiest bits of jam, the prettiest you'll ever see, present company excepted."

Mary bumps Parm with her shoulder, sending his hat flying. Eyelashes fluttering, she pretends outrage. "Why Parm, how can you say such awful things?"

What is the matter with Mary? Who is this swoony girl? Where did my old friend go?

✳ ✳ ✳

On the first day of school, I'm dressed hours early. After a careful inspection, Mama goes through her jewelry box, selecting a simple silver brooch. Centering it in my blouse's collar, she steps back. "The finishing touch. You look lovely."

Mary and George are waiting for me in front of the McLeans' house.

As we near the school, the sidewalk fills with other pupils. There are shouts and greetings. The high school building, three stories high, looms in front of us—an American flag fluttering from a small lookout tower on the top. A low picket fence surrounds the entire property. For the past three years, Mary and I entered the building from the back. Today, we go through the front as official high school students.

"Whew, lots of kids," George mumbles.

Mary lowers her voice. "Over five hundred."

And all taller than me, even with my new boots. Will it always be like this? Even Emma is taller.

The second-floor balcony is chock-full of boys and girls yelling and laughing. Red and white paper chains drape the railing.

George shakes his head. "Now there's one jolly group."

"Seniors. Do you see Parm?"

"There he is," Mary shouts, jumping up and down, waving. Parm waves back.

"He adores all this senior hoopla," I explain to George. "He even convinced my mother to knit a red-and-white scarf for him."

"Our class colors will be prettier," Mary says, hooking her arm through George's. "Each class gets to do things like that. Choose colors, write class songs and class mottos. You'll see."

I forgot about this part of high school. School spirit, they call it. I plan to leave this to the others.

Chapter 10

A MOMENT IN TIME

The first thing I notice about high school is that the teachers don't coddle us. And, of course, we're allowed to come and go as we please. There is also something called *school spirit*, which to me sounds like a waste of time.

I run into Mary before lunch. She grabs my hand.

"You've got to come to the class meeting, Julia. Everyone'll be there."

"I don't know, Mary."

"Oh, come on. One hour. For me?" she pleads.

"But..."

"Just this once. You won't be sorry."

But of course, I'm sorry. Afterwards, as we race to our next class, I list my complaints to Mary. "Number one, the boys took over the meeting. Number two, all our newly elected class officers are boys. Number three, I'm tired of listening to them. When they weren't making silly jokes, they were giving too many flowery speeches."

"You're right, Julia. Still, the Picnic Basket Social sounds like fun."

"I suppose."

My thoughts are already focused on the class I have been looking forward to all day—mechanical drawing. I double-check the sign on the door.

ROOM 105
MISS CONNORS
DRAWING CLASS

Inside are rows of stools lined up in front of drafting tables, tops slanting downwards. On my way to the girls' side of the room, my good spirits sag. Those stools. How will I climb to the top without looking foolish?

A freckle-faced boy, bow tie off-kilter, blocks my way. "Are you lost, little girl? This is the high school. Irving's that way."

"Is this the drafting class?"

"Sure thing."

"Then, yes, this *is* the place for me."

"Really?" He lifts an eyebrow. "Well, good luck then."

While Miss Connors waits at the front of the class-room, I study this famous teacher said to be fiercely demanding. I expected a giant. Instead, she's my height—no more than five feet. Her blue eyes scan the room, appraising us, one by one.

"All right, class. You may be seated."

As I feared, it takes several attempts for me to climb atop the stool. I ignore the snickering, even when my boot heel catches on the lower rim.

At roll call, Miss Connors pauses at my name.

"Julia Morgan?" she asks a second time, scanning the room for me.

"Yes, ma'am," I repeat louder, sliding off my stool to stand.

"Is your brother Parmelee Morgan?"

"Yes, ma'am."

"Ah. I remember him." In the silence that follows, I wonder if she remembers him in a good or bad way. Her sigh before moving to the next name confirms my hunch. During those few days Parmelee attended Miss Connors's mechanical drawing class, his complaints were loud and frequent. When he finally gave up, he declared the class "too boring."

While Miss Connors speaks, the room is silent. No shuffling of feet or even a cough. "Today we shall cover orthographic projections and the elements of isometric solids. Simply put, we shall begin by drawing stairs. Please take out your tools."

During the next hour I make a surprising discovery. The moment my pencil touches the paper, I can envision the completed staircase down to the smallest detail. As I measure and draw my lines, I see the stairway curve and climb upwards, then twist back down.

Miss Connors wanders from desk to desk, offering suggestions. At the end of the hour, she delivers a short speech.

"The work here is challenging. Not all of you will succeed. Some will find you have neither the skill nor the inclination to master mechanical drawing. The sooner you learn that, the better. Those who stay for all three years will be well prepared to become electrical or mechanical engineers, designers, or architects. I use the three *P*'s to describe what we do here. Perspective. Proportion. Precision. Only the most capable of you will advance. Expect daily homework."

Homework? Every night? Even on Mondays and Wednesdays? How will I manage this when Emma and I will be at the Simmons Dancing Academy learning the waltz, two-step, polka, and gavotte?

That afternoon, while Mama embroiders tiny red and white flowers on a new set of cloth napkins, I plead my case. "You can't imagine the stacks of homework."

"I can, Dudu." I watch her needle.

"But these dancing lessons! How do you expect...?"

The needle speeds up.

"I thought we settled this, daughter. While schoolwork is important, you absolutely must be ready for the season."

The Season. How I loathe those words. From May to December, all well-to-do Oakland girls and boys attend a series of balls, ending with the grandest of all, the debutante ball. And why? So that the best families can announce to the world: *Eligible young men—apply here to compete for the hand of my beautiful and charming daughter.* Even though my "coming out" is not until my last year of high school, Mama is already making plans to ensure I'm ready.

"Mama, please. I have no interest in any of this."

"You're only fifteen, Dudu. How do you know what you want?"

This is how all our conversations end lately. I swallow my objections. It will only make Mama furious if I tell her how little I care about endless rounds of parties, fancy dress-up balls, and empty-headed boys.

Naturally, I lose the dance lesson battle, but thanks to Mary, my first dance class is a cackle. Her attempts to dance with handsome George couldn't have been more entertaining.

"All right, everyone, line up. Boys on one side, girls on the other," Mr. Simmons instructs. "Now that you know the steps, we shall try the waltz in couples."

I watch Mary count off to George's spot in the boys' line before taking her place in the girls' line. Once I saw her squeeze between two girls. They were not happy. Most of the time Mary's strategy works and George becomes her partner. Maybe I should follow her lead. The boys I end up with tower above me and have such sweaty hands I need a towel to dry off.

Later that night, I face a pile of homework, including Miss Connors's assignment. I decide to do the least interesting first—reading Plutarch, the Greek philosopher. Convinced he will be as dry as dust, I'm surprised to find otherwise. While plowing through the first chapter, a single line leaps out. I like it so much I write it out in my own words.

"The whole of life is but a moment of time. It is our duty, therefore, to use it, not to misuse it."
—Plutarch

How do I convince Mama that debutante balls are a waste of my "moment of time"? Plutarch is right. Life is brief, and I plan to make the most of mine. Dancing, meeting boys, and fussing over how I look feels like misusing life rather than using it well.

By midnight, I reward myself for finishing everything by rereading Cousin Pierre's amusing letter.

September 15, 1887

Dear Julia,
Lady Liberty continues to command our atten-
tion here, but you'll never guess why. It appears
that she is massacring hundreds of birds, or as
the newspaper says, "Dashing Out Their Lives."
It happens at night, especially during storms. The
glare of the electric lamps in Lady Liberty's torch
and around the base of the pedestal blind the poor
things. Fortunately, death is quick. Their little
bodies are collected in the morning either on the
balcony or around the pedestal. Last week during
a powerful storm, 1,300 feathered friends met
their demise by flying into the statue.
*   The question of what to do with the tiny*
corpses led to a spirited discussion. Many of our
city's milliners are willing to pay a pretty penny for
them. As you know, the ladies are fond of deco-
rating their bonnets with birds. But the authorities
have decided to send the bodies to Washington's
Smithsonian Institution for counting, etc. A good
solution that ended the bickering amongst the
city's milliners for purchasing rights. Cousin Lucy,
however, is not happy with the outcome, especially
after she learned that wrens and whippoorwills,
prized for bonnets, were among the little victims.

I'm sure Plutarch would use this letter as evidence of
how we humans waste time doing silly things, all for a
pretty hat.

* * *

Fall semester speeds ahead. We move from Greek philosophers to Roman conquests. Algebra and geography hardly challenge me. Latin is easy. Mechanical drawing is another matter. Most nights I stay up late working on those assignments, mainly because I cannot stop. I'm lost in a world I never want to leave. Night after night I work long and late. The lack of sleep is of no consequence.

Mama, however, is not pleased. "Dudu, you were up late again. I saw your light."

"Yes, ma'am."

"Is the work too difficult?"

"No, of course not."

"What is it then? What keeps you up so late?"

What do I say? I turn a simple assignment into a complicated challenge, mainly because I see so many ways to complete it. Should I tell her how it feels to hold a newly sharpened pencil? How I lose track of time? How everything slips from sight and sound, except for my work? If I dare to explain, would Mama give me that look? The one that says, "Dudu. Such nonsense."

Unfortunately, I also lose all track of time in class, which is when Miss Connors taps me on the shoulder. "Julia, I asked the class to stop."

I glance around. Everyone is staring, some are snickering. My cheeks burn.

"Sorry, Miss Connors," I mumble, taking a last look at my incomplete work. The wait to finish a drawing at home is agonizing.

Chapter 11

TOO BRAINY

As the months fly by, I establish a routine that my parents accept. After the last bite of dessert, I race upstairs to do my homework. One night, however, Papa brings up a subject at the dinner table that has been bothering him—our crowded schools. Everyone wants a say, even little Sam.

"Today my teacher called me Jonathan," he pouts. "I'm nearly in the third grade, and she still doesn't know my name." He slumps in his chair, arms crossed.

Mama eyes Sam. "Sit up straight, young man. No slouching."

Avery is no happier. "Have you looked inside a classroom, Mama? Two kids to a desk. With fifty of us in the room, we can barely move."

Predictably, Papa's interest has to do with money. "Here we are in Ward Three paying the highest taxes in the city, but the classrooms are jam-packed. And we have to squeeze our grammar school into the high school. The incompetent school board promises to build us one, eventually, but we're still waiting. Something should be done."

"None of this concerns me, you know," Parm gloats. My stomach tightens. I know what's coming. "When I graduate this May, I'll never have to sit in a classroom again."

Everyone is still. This topic never ends well.

"And what do you plan to do, son? I don't mind your not going to college. It's not for everyone. But you need a plan, and all I've heard so far is what you're *not* going to do. Why, when I was your age . . . "

"But I'm not you, Papa," Parmelee interrupts.

No one notices my silent exit as Papa and Parm launch into their familiar quarrel.

Sitting at my desk, I debate which assignment to work on first. Miss Connors's drawing assignment wins. We are to create a bird's-eye view of any building we choose as long as we can see it from our school's tower. The tower, with windows on all four sides, offers a fine view of the city. After considering several sites, I decide on an unusual structure I walk by all the time.

The next day, as I climb the tower's narrow staircase, voices and thumping noises dash my hope of being alone. The room is packed with fellow drawing students. As soon as I step inside, the place turns eerily quiet.

I'm not surprised. The boys have never approved of me. Pencils go missing from my desk, my work is crumpled or tossed to the floor, and every day my stool mysteriously moves to the back of the room. It hardly ever happens to the few girls in the class. Just me. Although I hate the situation, it would be worse if I spoke up. Over the years, I've grown used to being teased by both boys and girls, mainly about my good grades. But high school is different. The boys in mechanical drawing have made it clear: I am not welcome.

I make my way to the best window for viewing my subject—the Pardee water tower. It's a two-story wood construction, wider at the bottom, and topped with a windmill. Two boys standing by the window appear absorbed in their drawings. When I head toward a second, less favorable window, the boys standing there act as if I'm invisible. The air in this crowded, silent room is stale and unpleasant, much like the smell of dirty laundry in my brothers' bedroom.

Heading to a third window, I steel myself for trouble, resolving to be sugar sweet. I will shame them. With a cheery smile, I say, "Excuse me. Is there room for one more here?"

The boy with freckles finally looks up from his sketchpad. "Have to wait 'til we're done. And that could take a while." I glance at his notebook. Blank.

I want to race back down those stairs, but I stay. Still smiling, I say, "Frankly, I think your estimate is incorrect. I shall not take up much room."

If they are like my brothers, they will back down like timid deer. Can they hear the frantic flutter in my chest? After the briefest pause, they shuffle aside, red-faced, leaving me a tiny space.

The water tower is visible against a flame-red sunset. Within minutes I have a decent rendering. A quick glance at the boys' sketchbooks confirms my hunch. Still blank.

The floorboards creak as I leave the church-quiet room. Reaching the bottom of the stairs, I hear that familiar refrain. "She's too brainy for a girl."

The laughter that follows stings worse than the words. I shut the door behind me, angry. What's wrong with a girl being smarter than a boy? And so what if I draw well? It's easy for me, like breathing.

Over the next months, matters get worse, but I develop a survival strategy. Keep quiet. Do good work. Mind my own business. Before I know it, the year is over, Parm graduates, and I make the honor roll. Summer promises a brief relief from my torment.

Chapter 12

A MAN WITH A MISSION

At the start of summer vacation, Mama urges Mary and me to work on our needlepoint. "A little every day," she insists. "How else do you expect to fill your hope chest before you marry?" Leave it to Mama to remind us of such matters.

Even so, while we work I enjoy listening to Mary's chatter, but first she asks about Parm's high school graduation. When I describe my parents' relief that their eldest son received his diploma, she nods knowingly.

Not surprisingly, Mary prefers talking about George. "Those last months of school, he was working like a dog. You saw the change in him, didn't you? His smile? Gone."

"I didn't know he was having such a hard time," I admit.

"How could you *not* notice?"

Mary's reaction hurts. I was unaware of George's academic predicament. I admonish myself to be extra attentive.

"His grades are poor Julia, and his final exams were pitiful."

I am understanding. "It's a challenging school."

"Yes, that's true. It's obvious his Hawaiian tutors let him down. He was unprepared for a mainland education. But Julia . . . "

I look up from my sampler, needle still. I am attentive.

"I have a confession to make."

"Yes?"

"I should be more upset. He had his heart set on going to an eastern college this fall."

I am consoling. "He'll go. Just not this year."

"Perhaps. But all I can think about is how lucky I am. Is that mean of me?" Mary tries to hold back her smile.

"A little."

"Oh, I suppose you're right. Still, isn't he a dream? Have you seen how he looks at me?"

"Of course," I fib, having not witnessed such behavior.

"He doesn't stare, but he looks at me when he thinks I don't notice. I'm certain he's fond of . . . Ouch!"

Predictably, Mary's thimble fails to protect her from the needle. Sucking on her finger to stop the bleeding, she asks the question I've been dreading. "Have you spoken to your mother about your coming out?"

"No. Not yet. I've come close, though," Another fib. I have deliberately avoided talking to Mama about debutante parties.

"Julia, you absolutely must, and soon. The other mothers are already planning for the big ball. Tell her."

"But how? What do I say?"

Both our needles stop. I go on. "If this was about one big party, I would happily agree. But you know that's not how it works. It's all those other parties . . . dozens of them . . . dancing with those boys shopping for future brides. No, Mary. I have no desire to become a debutante. None whatsoever."

"Never?"

"Never! And I simply don't understand how you can."

"It's easy. It's all about pleasing my parents. I'm an only child. My coming out means a lot to them. You're lucky, Julia. You have Emma. She can't wait for all of this."

Her words are like beams of sparkling light.

"Say that again, Mary."

"You have Emma."

"That's it! Emma!" I say louder than I intended.

Mary, perplexed, rubs her temple.

"Don't you get it, Mary?"

She shakes her head. "Not at all."

"All I have to do is convince Mama to skip me and concentrate on Emma."

"You're smart, Julia, but not *that* smart."

She may be right. Convincing Mama of anything is like carrying water in a strainer—impossible. And then there is Grandmother, fiercely opposed to shirking one's social duties. Still, I have a whole year until the party season for my age group starts—plenty of time to convince Mama that Emma is better suited for a coming-out party.

We are interrupted by Papa stomping into the parlor, followed by Mama. His cherry-red complexion is alarming.

"I'm against it, I tell you." he shouts. "The school board is wrong. Moving Irving students from our over-crowded high school to Tompkins Grammar School on the other side of town is no solution. I won't have it. Ward

Three needs its own grammar school. Right here. In our own neighborhood."

Over the next several weeks, all Papa can talk about is the Tompkins business, especially the rumors of its unhealthy location.

"It's surrounded by stagnant, disease-carrying water. Mark my words. No child of mine is going to step foot in that cesspool," he thunders.

Soon there are near-nightly gatherings in our front parlor. The fired-up parents of Ward Three prepare for battle at the next school board meeting, with Papa as their leader.

"I think I'll go," I tell Mama.

"Parmelee is, but why is beyond me," she responds.

I find out soon enough.

Angry parents fill the hall, made grumpier by the steamy, hot weather—summer's last gasp. The boa-tight corset squeezing my ribs adds to my misery.

Parmelee brings a crowd of raucous boys from his graduating class. For them, this is their evening's entertainment. I sit near the women, within easy reach of the water pitchers. With so many fans in motion, mine is unnecessary.

As the evening wears on, the parents give the speeches they prepared in our parlor. Finally, it's Papa's turn. He starts slowly, softly, but soon his words vibrate throughout the hall. I have never seen him like this. While he may get excited about things at home, tonight he is transformed into a first-class speaker.

When the applause dies down, the president calls for the vote.

At breakfast the next morning, Papa is so excited, he eats all the toast. "Marvelous evening. We made our case crystal clear," he says, spreading marmalade on the last piece.

"You should have seen him," I squeeze in. "It was unanimous. The entire Board voted yes on his idea to keep Ward Three kids here, instead of moving them to Tompkins."

"They did indeed. What a night!" Papa gloats.

"I'm relieved, dear," Mama says. "Tompkins. So far away, and so unhealthy."

"But, Liza, they have a smart principal. I met him last night before the meeting. His name is Edwin Markham. A poet, too. Nice chap."

"That may be, Charles, but I'm glad our children won't be going to his school." Mama studies Papa. "You know dear, I haven't seen you so high-spirited in quite some time."

"All this school business is a nice change of pace, and frankly, I'm good at it. Managing the iron foundry is fine, but politics agrees with me. Some are saying I should make a run for the school board position."

Papa unbuttons his jacket, making room for that last piece of toast.

* * *

Weeks later, when Papa throws his hat into the political ring, he becomes a whirlwind of energy. Has he been hiding this part of his personality from us all along? I thought I was the only Morgan deceiving the world. On the outside I'm the dutiful daughter who excels in school. But I, too, am wearing a mask, hiding a dream. I have not told Mary yet. Indeed, I'm not sure how, but Papa has inspired me.

Chapter 13

THREE SHRILL RINGS

The second year of high school is as demanding as the first. Most challenging? French. Most enjoyable? Mechanical drawing, of course.

This year the focus is about lines, shapes, and perspective. I spend far too many hours copying the models that Miss Connors stores in the school's attic. Most other pupils grumble about the assignment, but I relish the challenge of creating exact, precise images. My detailed drawing of an elaborate corner molding got the highest grade. On my paper, Miss Connors wrote, *I feel as if I can reach out and touch it.*

Most confusing class? English.

Fortunately, George and Mary are taking it, too. This week we are reading Shakespeare's *Julius Caesar.*

"Why doesn't Shakespeare say what he means?" George gripes after yet another head-spinning class. "Why doesn't he explain things more clearly and to the point?"

"I can help you, George," Mary shouts, as we push our way through the crowded, noisy halls, huddled together like birds in a windstorm.

"Why did Brutus kill Caesar?" George hollers above the racket.

"He was a dictator," I shout over my shoulder as I head to algebra with Mr. Chambers, a real-life dictator. No teacher is tougher or more demanding. Still, algebra is another of my favorites.

At lunchtime, I eat outside with members of the Girls Debate Society. They are still heated up about their last debate topic—the danger of rumors.

"Here's an example for you," says Bertie Shrader, the Society's outspoken president. "Did you read that newspaper article claiming that rich girls in our school show off by wearing diamonds and silk?"

There were murmurs of agreement, heads nodding.

"We all know that's not true," she snorts. "Shows how dangerous rumors can be."

"Too ridiculous for words," says a girl in the back.

"Ladies," Bertie says. "We have more important matters to talk about than diamonds and silk. Our spring ride."

As a non-member, I back away. Bertie notices.

"Stay, Julia. This is for everyone, including you!"

The other girls nod. I have heard about the big ride from Mary, who plans to go.

"I've located a few tandem bikes, but I need your help," Bertie says. "We need more. Talk to everyone you know. Tell them it's scheduled for March, after the worst of the rainy season. Invite your friends, especially if they own one of these contraptions."

Most of these tandem bicycles hold two riders. Even though they are the latest rage, they're rare. I have always wanted to try one.

Miraculously, we locate thirteen tandems for all twenty-six of us. Our destination is picturesque Blair Park. Mary is paired with Alice Bailey. My partner is Gertrude Stein, a first-year student. We were matched up because of our similar height. This diversion could not come at a better time. I need a break from the grind of school.

The ride is amusing, especially when we make a wrong turn. There's lots of maneuvering and shouting, until we get back on course. Gertrude is an ideal partner. She chooses the front seat but doesn't mind taking directions from me in the back like "slow down," or "lean right," or "horse manure on the left."

We spread blankets under a stand of oak trees and enjoy our lunch with a clear view of the bay. On the ride home we sing loudly.

"Oh, I went down south for to see my Sal,
Singing Polly Wolly doodle all the day.
My Sal she is a spunky gal,
Play Polly Wolly doodle all the day."

The singing, the ride, the silliness, energizes me. I race up our porch steps two at a time. Throwing open the front door, I find the Morgan household in a tizzy. Tomorrow is Oakland's Election Day, and Papa hopes to be elected as the newest member of our school board.

He sits in his office, writing notes to our neighbors, asking for their vote. Mama is writing her friends. A sense of urgency engulfs the room. Avery and Emma stand nearby, waiting.

"Here, Avery," Papa says, handing him an envelope. "You know the Simpsons. Now step on it."

Avery races out the front door. Emma is next in line. The front door slams. It's Sam.

"Back Papa. Ready for the next one," he shouts, saluting smartly.

Papa is making good use of this last day. By the end of the week, after all the votes are counted, it is official. Papa wins!

There is hardly a second to celebrate. Miss Connors assigns a new and challenging project. By now, I'm familiar with her methods. Two drawings are pinned up in the classroom, side by side.

"This is what I want you to think about," Miss Connors says, holding a long wooden pointer. "Both of these designs were created by the French engineer, Gustave Eiffel. I know you'll recognize this one."

When her pointer touches the drawing of the Liberty statue, the room buzzes.

"You may be less familiar with the other."

I recognize it immediately. It's Mr. Eiffel's latest project, due to be finished next year—a tower for the World Exposition in Paris. Eiffel is the same engineer who designed the "skeleton" for the Liberty statue.

"Your job is to prepare a series of drawings that compare these structures—six sketches for each. Include notes on the materials Eiffel uses, and explain what you think influenced his choices. For example, both structures are extremely tall. Both will be exposed to heavy wind, severe cold, heat, and weathering. I'm aware that this assignment reaches beyond what you've learned in my class, but I want to see how you build on what we have studied thus far. Turn in your work by April 10. Late work will not be accepted."

Cousin Pierre and I have exchanged letters about Gustave Eiffel. In one he described how Eiffel's iron foundry creates new and startling shapes, unlike Papa's, which produces everyday pieces like bolts and screws.

After class, I stand next to Arthur Brown in front of the drawings. He's the only boy in class who is decent to me, never stepping on my work when it mysteriously slides off my drawing board. He dresses nicely, and his hair is always parted neatly in the middle. He works hard and does well. A first-year pupil who is crystal clear about his future. He wants to be an architect, like his dad. How did he decide?

Most of the time I prefer listening rather than talking. This time I surprise myself by speaking my thoughts aloud. "I wonder why Mr. Eiffel chose steel for the Liberty skeleton, and iron for his tower."

Arthur has questions, too. "I want to know how he designed the Liberty skeleton. How did he connect the thin outer copper skin to the inside supports?"

I tell Arthur what I know about Eiffel's design for the statue. By the time we go our separate ways, I know what to do.

That night, I reread Cousin Pierre's letter, skipping down to the part about his skyscraper.

As I've always said, steel worked for the Brooklyn Bridge, and for the Liberty statue's armature. It can take that powerful East River wind. And structures need to sway a little and hold up under damp winters. The same applies to skyscrapers. And don't forget, steel is light and strong, which means my walls can weigh less, reducing the stress.

I work hard on my drawings, completing twice as many as required. Miss Connors is strict about deadlines, so I bring my work to school two days before the April deadline. Besides, getting it out of the house will stop me from making more changes.

That night, Mama asks for my help balling new yarn. I hold up my hands, palms facing each other. She sets the red wool on them. Sitting in front of her like this, I decide to raise the delicate subject of the debutante ball. Whenever I tried in the past, she refused to listen.

I'm stunned when she beats me to it. "Dudu, about your coming-out party. Before we know it, the season will be upon us. The other mothers and I agree about which hall to rent. If only we can . . . "

"Mama."

"Don't interrupt, dear."

"But, Mama. It's important."

I look at her face, so near mine. New lines fan out from the corners of her eyes.

She sighs. "All right, Dudu. But I don't see what could be more important."

I plunge on. "I've told you before. I don't have time for such matters. You know my studies are demanding. Besides, there's plenty of time to meet young men."

"I won't hear this, Dudu."

If she could plug her ears to block out my voice, she would.

"But, Mama . . . "

"You know very well that such conduct could spoil your chances of finding a husband. I will not let that happen. It's time you face the facts. You have obligations. The sooner you accept that, the better."

"But . . . "

"No. It's out of the question. And I'm not alone. Your grandmother would be shocked."

When Mama pauses for breath, I jump in. "You've forgotten something important, Mama."

"Fiddlesticks!"

"What about Emma?"

"Emma? Whatever do you mean?"

"You know Emma can't wait for her coming out. You've heard her go on about the gown she'll wear, the young men she'll meet, and the whirl of parties. In a few years, you can put all your effort into Emma. Make sure her coming out is wonderful. On the other hand, I'm certain to disappoint you."

"Nonsense."

"Mama, we have to be realistic. I'm not as pretty as Emma. I don't dance nearly as well. And you know my heart isn't in it."

Before Mama can respond, three bells jangle noisily outside. There is a moment of silence, followed by the sound of three more bells. Mama and I look at each other. Three bells. Fire in Ward Three.

Seconds later more bells ring throughout our neighborhood.

Chapter 14

ALL ASHES

S am races into the parlor, his cheeks as red as ripe apples. "A fire. It's a fire! Let's go see."

When Mama pulls aside the parlor curtain, I peer over her shoulder. "It does sound close," I say.

"Come on," Sam urges, running to the front door. "Hurry."

The street is already filled with curious neighbors. Sam tugs my hand. "Let's go. Please, please," he begs.

Mama eyes Sam. "Now listen here, young man. You may go but stay with your sister. Do you hear me? And before you take another step, put on your wraps—both of you."

Mama is a real softie with Sam. Removing her shawl, she hands it to me.

Sam grabs his cap and jacket. "Hurry, Dudu. We'll miss everything."

Soon, we are swept along with our neighbors, all heading downtown. We had only gone a few blocks when Sam shouts, "Look! The fire! I see it."

An unnatural light brightens the night sky. There are shouts. "The school! The high school's on fire!"

I hurry on. Curiosity turning into urgency. Two blocks later I have a clear view. Orange and red flames shoot out of my school's third-story window.

Sam and I are at the back of the crowd, but soon hundreds more people crowd behind us.

"Look, look," he shouts. "The roof. Flames! I see the flames. But I can't see the engines. I want to see the engines." He drops my hand, taking off before I can grab him.

"Sam! Come back."

He doesn't stop. My yell—muffled by the crowd, sirens, bells, and firemen's shouts—has no effect on slowing down the little rascal. Everything about firemen fascinates Sam. He disappears into the crowd.

Frantically, I push my way to the front, passing the tired horses guarded by a pair of black-and-white Dalmatians. Sam is standing by the pumper truck, water surging through its hoses. A policeman blocks his way. When I grab Sam's hand, he hardly notices.

Hoses are strewn about the ground like a giant spider web. Several ladders lean against the wood frame building. Firemen stand on the top rungs, hoses in hand. More flames leap from the roof.

When a team of horses pulls up with a fourth hook and ladder, Sam squeezes my hand. "The ladders! Aren't they the best?"

Just then a fireman on a ladder in front of us loses his footing. Falling sideways, he hits a second-story awning before plummeting to the ground. Everyone gasps. I cover Sam's eyes. He tears my hand away. The crowd is silent.

Several firemen huddle around the man's still body. After an agonizing wait, the fireman kneeling beside the fallen man waves both arms above his head. The crowd cheers, Sam loudest of all.

Minutes later, there is a second calamity. A chunk of carved wood breaks loose from a corner of the building, falling on an unlucky fireman. Blood streams down his face. He shakes his head, looking up with a stunned expression. Someone presses a rag to the gash on his forehead. With the help of a man on either side, he walks unsteadily to one of the engines but stops to wave at the crowd before a fellow fireman makes him sit down. Everyone cheers a second time.

The decorative wood piece that clobbered the poor man is supposed to resemble carved stone. Some people like the elaborate carvings. Now, watching all those wood ornaments burn, I have little doubt that a real stone structure would be far superior.

Eventually, the bright flames turn into long plumes of gray smoke, blotting out the starry sky. The third floor is all but gone. Until that moment, I didn't give a thought to how the fire could affect me. Now I wonder. Where will we have classes? How long will it take before we can return to our building?

As the firemen begin rolling up their hoses, I realize something terrible. My project for Miss Connors's class, the one I labored over for so long, is now either a pile of ashes or a soggy mess. I feel as if I've been soaked by a fireman's hose.

Sam huddles close. "I'm getting cold."

"Me, too. Let's go." I'm shivering, but not from the

cool night air. Sam babbles all the way home. His voice fades as my mind races.

* * *

That Saturday, Papa attends a school board meeting about the fire. On Monday, we gather with our teachers in Hamilton Hall to learn our fate.

The school board president speaks first. "We'll try to put you some place reasonably convenient," he promises.

"I can imagine where that'll be," George mutters from his place on my right. "Wagner's Smoke House, most likely, next to the ham, bacon, and pork."

Mary, on my other side, covers her mouth, suppressing a giggle. "My word, George. Where do you get such outlandish ideas?" She still has hopes for George.

The school superintendent admits they have no definite plan, but he tells a story to boost our spirits. "This morning I met a gentleman on the street. He said to me, 'So, your high school is gone.' I replied, 'No, sir. Fires may come and fires may go, but the high school will continue on just the same.'"

The hall echoes with applause and stamping feet. The superintendent smiles as he waits for the room to quiet. Pointing to the front row, he says. "Now, these teachers here are all that's left of your school." The room once again erupts with applause. "But it's the best school in the world because you have Mr. McChesney as your principal along with these fine teachers. The Board of Education stands ready to meet this emergency. Do your part, and we'll do ours."

It is now Mr. McChesney's turn. "You all know it's not the building that makes the school. Right?" Some of the boys take this as a cue for more foot stomping and hooting. Mr. McChesney waits. "But I promise you that the seniors will indeed graduate. For those of you who lost work in the fire, I'm afraid you'll have to redo it."

I groan. Mary and George place an arm over my shoulders. Mr. McChesney ends with a few words about the possibility of building a new high school. From Papa I know this issue led to heated debate. Repair the old building or build a new one? Papa is firmly on the side of building a new one.

After the meeting I catch Miss Connors on her way out. Several other pupils cluster around her.

"Miss Connors. I . . . "

"Yes, I know Miss Morgan. Your project. You'll have to do it over."

I search her face for the hint of a smile, that she's joking. How can I do this assignment a second time? I spent hours on those drawings, some of my best work. I will never be able to duplicate them.

She looks at the other students. "That goes for all of you who were as diligent as Miss Morgan. You have one week. And I'm sorry. Everything is gone . . . ashes. My books, too. All gone." Miss Connors shakes her head as she slowly leaves the hall.

That afternoon, hoping Mama will notice my drawing skills, which are far better than my dancing skills, I start a new set of drawings on the parlor table. Before my pencil touches paper, I sit quietly, erasing all thoughts of my ruined assignment. I resolve that these new drawings will be more detailed, precise, and intricate. Absorbed in measuring angles and drawing lines, Papa startles me by waving around a copy of the *Oakland Tribune*.

"Dudu, listen to this. I couldn't say it better." He adjusts his glasses. "It's an article about Oakland High. The writer calls the building design a failure—a bad example of the worst period in American architecture. The chap's right, you know. He complains that the school is a poor copy of the Europe's stone architecture but in wood. *Pretentious*, he calls it. *An architectural sham.* Listen to this. *The only good thing about such a building is that when it catches fire, it burns to the ground in a half hour.*"

"May I see that, Papa?"

"Yes. But read it aloud. I'm quite enjoying it."

I pick up from where he left off. "*Building lofty wooden structures for school purposes is a serious and dangerous mistake. My only hope is that they hire some-one to build a new high school using stone.*"

With every sentence Papa nods in agreement. "No question I'm going to use this editorial at our next board meeting."

Papa's keen on a new building, and I agree with him. The high school is a monstrosity. If I had my way, I'd tear the thing down. The design is all wrong, and completely impractical.

Unfortunately, he loses the battle. The board decides to rebuild our school by removing the fire-damaged third floor and then cleaning and expanding the bottom two floors. The work should be finished by next October. The only good news is that we'll be back in the building for my senior year.

In the meantime, classes meet in three places down-town—Hamilton Hall, the Seventh-day Adventist Church, and the Hebrew Synagogue, all within a block of each other.

The worst part of the arrangement is racing between the three buildings. Rain makes a difficult situation mis-erable. To avoid the mud, we walk across several planks placed on the ground in the worst spots, but lack of desks is a problem. The solution? More planks supported by sawhorses.

Mary especially hates the new rules slapped on us. "They're stricter than before," she complains as we trudge through April showers. "Like that rule about girls walking on Broadway. Only groups of four. How ridiculous!"

Avoiding a mud puddle, I bump Mary. "Oops. Sorry."

She barely notices. "It's so we don't block people on the sidewalks," I say. "There really are a lot of us out and about these days."

"Oh, Julia. Don't be so sensible."

Despite these challenges, I finish the year with high marks. At our final assembly, each teacher presents letters of commendation to their outstanding students.

Tenth grade pupils are up first. Miss Fisher awards my biking partner, Gertrude Stein, a commendation for her essay on "seeing." The topic perplexes me, but apparently not Miss Fisher.

When it's Miss Connors's turn, I'm astonished to hear her call my name. As I stand in front of everyone, she unfolds a piece of paper, and reads aloud.

"Miss Morgan has shown considerable talent on a chal-lenging assignment regarding the engineer Gustave Eiffel. She has also demonstrated praiseworthy determination.

Although she lost her first assignment in the fire, her re-creation was exceptional."

As I return to my seat, letter clutched in my hands, I note the girls' smiles and the boys' frowns.

Mary and I celebrate the end of the school year with cold lemonade in the shade of our backyard gazebo. "Our first lazy day of summer," she says, grinning.

A single crow scolds us. I'm sure he is admonishing me. I deserve it. Mary and I promised each other that we would always be honest with each another. But I've kept something from her, a secret. The commendation gives me newfound confidence.

"I'm at a crossroads, Mary."

"Ohhhh. Let me guess. You've decided on new wall-paper for your bedroom. I know you dislike too many flowers, and frankly, I agree."

"Think bigger, Mary. Much, much bigger."

"Come on, Julia. Just tell me."

"It's a decision I've made about college, that is if I go."

"Oh, you'll go, and I will too. I'm sure."

"What do you want to study?"

"Literature. No question. I can't wait." Mary looks my way. "I hear the French department is good, Julia. You might like that."

"No. Not French."

"What then?"

"I have something else in mind. And frankly, asking my parents about college is the least of it. When I tell them what I want to study, they will not be happy."

"Spill the beans, Julia."

I take a deep breath.

"Engineering, Mary. That's what I want to study."

There, I've said it. She doesn't look surprised. Is that a good sign?

I hurry on. "Before you say anything, listen. I have no choice. Architecture is what I really want to study, but the university doesn't offer that so it's engineering for me."

I wait for her reaction. Will she think I'm crazy?

"Architecture? Really?"

"Really. There's nothing I'd rather do. Nothing."

Now that I have finally shared my secret aloud, I'm more determined than ever.

"Well, Julia . . . " Mary sips her lemonade. "I love the idea, but you'll never guess why."

I exhale. "Tell me."

"Someday, Miss Morgan, you're going to design a house for me."

Good old Mary. Always ready to leap into the next wonderful possibility.

"I'd be more than delighted, Miss McLean." And I mean it.

Chapter 15

EVERY GIRL'S DREAM

"Miss Connors thinks highly of you," Mama says closing her eyes and tilting her face toward the sun. We are sitting in the garden, enjoying the May weather. My letter of commendation rests in her lap. Grandmother naps on the wicker chaise lounge, a blanket tucked around her legs.

I hate to disturb this peaceful moment, but I have no choice. "Miss Connors says I have a natural ability for mechanical drawing. But she's warned me that next year will be even more demanding."

I don't tell Mama how Miss Connors thinks I should study engineering in college or how Pierre LeBrun agrees. With a mixture of fear and hope, I push on. "Frankly, Mama, my participation in the debutante ball presents a problem."

There, I said it. Mama's eyes flutter open.

"That is, if I hope to do well in my senior year."

"Dudu, we've already settled this. It's all about your prospects, about meeting the right young man, about your future. We do know what's best for you, young lady."

"But . . . "

"Naturally, this includes what every young girl desires. Marriage, children, a household to care for, a husband to look after. Don't you agree?"

"Yes, Mama," I say, stomach aching from my fib.

Can't you see, Mama? Those are your dreams, not mine. I don't want what you want. I wish I knew how to tell you.

Grandmother is no help. She's always on Mama's side. In her opinion, coming out, becoming a debutante, is the high point of a girl's life. She loves telling stories about the dances and parties that thrilled her as a young girl growing up in the south. "That's how I met your grand-father," she likes to remind me.

"We're only talking about one ball," I say, aware of the futility of my argument.

Mama's eyebrows arch, a sure sign she's losing patience. "Not just *any* ball, Dudu."

Smoothly, I switch to her favorite topic—Pierre LeBrun. Unlike Miss Connors, whom Mama refers to as "that-lady-teacher-who-will-never-find-a-husband," she admires our cousin.

"Perhaps drawing and designing are in my future. That's what Cousin Pierre says."

Mama clasps her hands, eyeing me closely. In his last letter he was insistent. *Follow your interests. You have a good hand and a good head. Most importantly, I can tell that you have the desire.*

I don't mention that. Instead I say, "I've sent Cousin Pierre some of my work. He thinks it's good."

I wait for her reaction, mouth dry. Lightly, she touches her lip with a finger. Mama may think we are talking about a silly coming-out party, but really, we are talking about my future. In Mama's vision of my future, good grades are of little consequence. In the future I see for myself, I am an architect. Mama doesn't know this.

Finally, she says, "I'm not surprised he likes your work. Your drawings are excellent."

"Mama, I'm certain you have my best interests at heart. But I'm not like Emma. You know that. There is nothing she loves more than being fitted for a new gown, or the excitement of a party. I, on the other hand, am a dreadful dancer and detest making small talk. I truly believe I would be an embarrassment."

"Dudu. I hardly think that would be the case."

If I cannot persuade Mama now, she will never agree to my more preposterous idea—attending college.

Squirrels chitter-chatter. Crows squawk their daily complaints.

"I agree with you, my dear," says Mama. "You are nothing like Emma."

Her words alert me that what I said about my sister may have been unkind.

Hastily I add, "She's extremely bright."

"That's true of all my children." Mama says, inspecting the button of her sleeve instead of me. Finally, she looks up. "But you are different from the others, Dudu. You seem to know what you want, although you never shout about it."

"Yes, ma'am."

My hopes float overhead like Papa's cigar rings, threatening to evaporate.

Hurry up! Hurry up! scolds a blue jay from a nearby oak branch.

Mama sighs. "In some ways, I suppose this could make my life easier. Except I'll have your grandmother to deal with. She'll be terribly disappointed."

Grandmother snores softly. My hands are clasped so tightly they throb. Is Mama agreeing with me?

A crow jumps onto the lawn, squawking angrily. I sit, motionless. Mama removes a hankie tucked into her dress sleeve. Gently, she pats her damp forehead.

With a sigh, she says, "Consider your coming-out party off the social calendar."

I force myself to stay calm. Perhaps I misheard. "What was that, Mama?"

"Don't make me repeat myself, Dudu."

I'm balanced on the edge of my chair, back ramrod straight. Her words have an odd effect. This is what I prayed for. Now that it is real, I have the sensation of my chair disappearing from beneath me. "Thank you, Mama, thank you."

While I'm relieved, I have a second request, something that may trouble my mother more than my absence from the ball. "I'm grateful, Mama. This will make my senior year much less trying. And doing well in school is important." My words tumble out. There is no turning back. "Miss Connors has strongly encouraged me to enroll in Berkeley's university. They have an engineering program she thinks would suit me."

Mama's hands fly up to her coiled braid. Patting it in place, she remains silent. I go on. "I'm one of her top students, Mama. You read her commendation. And I love the work. I know I can do it."

"College. Dudu, I don't know." The crease between her eyebrows deepens.

"But why?"

"Oh, it's not the work. It's all those other things."

"What other things?"

Her face pales. "Engineering. Isn't that a man's subject?"

"Mainly, yes. It is."

"Don't you see what that means? Imagine what that will be like."

"I have. I can do it. It's mostly boys in my classes now. I get the best grades."

"I've just said to you that it's not about the work."

I know what troubles her. The men might be unfriendly, even hostile in their men-only world. They will not like me invading their territory.

"Dudu. Be reasonable. All the girls I know who attend the university are there to become teachers. And teaching is such nice, respectable work before marriage. Don't you agree?"

"It is. But teaching isn't for me, Mama. I have no interest in it."

She shakes her head. "You could study music. Or art. But engineering? Such a waste."

"Not really. Not if I want to study architecture, which I do. Cousin Pierre believes engineering is an excellent background for architects."

This is the first time I mention architecture to Mama. Even the blue jays, crows, and squirrels quiet.

"Architecture? My word," she says, shaking her head.

The idea crystalized in Miss Connors classes, but the pieces of this puzzle have always been there. I simply needed time to fit them together. I sensed it during those lonely hours when I was confined to bed with scarlet fever, constructing wood structures with my blocks. I knew something awaited me on that glorious day with Cousin Pierre on the Brooklyn Bridge.

Two squirrels scamper on the branch overhead. Acorns rain down. One hits my nose. Our laughter breaks the silence.

Finally, Mama sighs. "I'm not completely surprised."

"Really?" A dozen acorns falling on my head couldn't be more astonishing.

"I do pay attention."

"Then I can go to college?"

"Possibly. Naturally, Papa has the last word on the matter."

"Yes, ma'am."

I know what Papa will say. He was the first to support my choice of the Scientific Track. He couldn't wait to help me choose my tools for mechanical design. He has always been interested in my projects and drawings. I long to do something crazy like somersaults on the gymnasium equipment.

But Mama isn't finished. "All I know is that you should be glad you have brothers."

"Glad to have brothers?" I almost laugh aloud. "And why is that?"

"Someone must escort you to school. You shall not travel on the trolley to Berkeley on your own."

Mama's sensibilities seem a small price to pay. I can contain myself no longer. Mama stiffly accepts my hug. Grandmother wakens, studies us, then shuts her eyes.

An hour later I write Cousin Pierre with my news. Even though Papa has yet to agree about college, I'm confident he will. As I reread my letter, I realize I have been impolite. It's all about me and my engineering studies. I have not asked about his skyscraper project. He's run into a problem. Too much underground water has slowed excavation to a crawl.

Just as I finish writing *How is the groundwater problem? I know how you hate to see work delayed. What is your solution?*, Mary knocks on my bedroom door.

Usually, I can guess her mood with a glance, but not today. She looks like my neighbor's cat, Bella, when she catches a bird—pleased yet guilty.

"What is it? What's happened?"

She heads for the rocker, barely sitting before exploding. "It's finally happened. George leaves next year for Columbia University in New York."

"I don't know what to say, Mary."

"It's what he's wanted all along."

I study her face for signs of despair but see none.

The rocker stills. "But there's good news, Julia. He invited me to the Senior Ball. We shall dance the night away."

"Oh, Mary, you did it!"

From the beginning, we knew George's stay was temporary. The invitation to his senior ball is a splendid storybook ending to her tale.

After Mary exhausts the subject of George, it is my turn. "I'm grateful to you Mary."

"Me?"

"Yes, you."

"For what?"

"I am happy to inform you that my coming-out party is officially off the social calendar. And I have you to thank. You and your idea about Emma. Brilliant Mary."

"My word. I am brilliant, aren't I?"

"Indeed."

Mary's face brightens. "Ah, this is grand. Now you'll have more time to help with my coming out! The hall is booked, and the mothers are narrowing down the orchestra list. Of course, I'll miss you being a part of it, but you'll be there, and that's what really counts."

The ball is scheduled the week before Christmas, which is also when we take our exams. My shoulders tighten. "It'll be a busy time for me, Mary."

"I know that, but you're never too busy for me, are you?"

"Never," I say, hoping I have not told a fib.

Chapter 16

MARY, THE DEBUTANTE

Miss Connors's warning about senior year is spot on. The work is punishing. As usual, the more difficult the challenge, the more I'm driven to succeed. While architecture is the main topic, mostly we study perspective, drawing objects so they look like they can leap off the page. Periodically I like to imagine drawing plans for a building, but then it's back to angles. And they are everywhere—corners, joints, ceilings, and stairs.

Of course, this would be easier in our school with our old drawing tables and stools. I console myself knowing that the workmen are nearly finished patching and mending. Despite the extensive repair, our school will never be a thing of beauty.

In late October, we walk into our restored high school. While I'm pleased, I must once again struggle to climb atop my drafting stool.

Two weeks later, Papa is telling us about his speech to the school board in which he urges them to offer younger pupils "practical" school subjects where they use their hands.

"You know, things like clay modeling, woodcarving, carpentry, and blacksmithing. They liked my idea. The vote was a unanimous yes," he gloats. "I have some other ideas, but this one . . . "

He's interrupted by fire bells clanging outside. Sam counts aloud. One . . . two . . . three. Silence. One . . . two . . . three. Silence. Fire in Ward Three. Again!

To my horror, the evening is a replay of last April's disastrous fire. Sam, Avery, Emma, Parm, and I huddle in front of the high school, flames again lighting up the night sky.

The next morning, the entire student body gathers in front of the blackened ruins. The bitter smell of scorched, wet wood fills our nostrils. Everyone is silent except for Arthur Brown. "Me and the fellas saved a lot of books, some desks, furniture from the south wing," he says. "Sorry to say, most of the junior and senior books are ashes."

Studying the building, I'm relieved. "This fire doesn't look as bad as the last one."

"From the outside, you are right, Julia. But inside's a different story. There's lots of water damage. The roof is redwood. It burns slowly. If the firemen knew that, they would have fought the fire differently, from the inside instead of from the outside. They would have used less water. Instead, they kept pouring water through a hole in the roof."

Mary quizzes Arthur as if he were an expert. While he points out various parts of the scorched building and suggests possible origins of the fire, a copy of the *Oakland Tribune* falls from his back pocket. Handing it back to him, I notice a front-page story of an interview with the building architect.

❖ ❖ ❖

Three days later, classes resume in our old setup. Once again, we scurry around like rats from building to building. School board bickering delays the start of repair work. The grim reality hits. There is no possibility the work will be finished in time for May graduation.

The teachers take no notice. Assignments pile up. I work hard, but something nags at me. Mary's coming-out party. Can I do it all? Assignments? Study for exams? Mary's big night?

One wet November day, racing to the Hebrew Synagogue for classes, Mary and I are caught in a sudden downpour. Rain pelts our faces.

"You'll never believe when Miss Connors's next assignment is due," I shout, water dripping from the tip of my nose. "The Monday after your coming-out party."

Mary peers from beneath her umbrella. Narrowing her eyes, she says, "Now hold on, Julia Morgan. Don't even think about missing my big night. At our last rehearsal, our curtsies were perfect. And Mother needs you. We've far too many boys."

"It's just a busy time, that's all," I say, shivering as water trickles into my boots.

"Believe me, I know about being busy."

"I'll be there, Mary. Promise."

Can I keep my word? I try, but despite working late every night, assignments pile up. The Scientific Track is merciless. If I'm honest, this conundrum is of my own making—my need to excel. I will not turn in a paper or assignment until I'm sure it is perfect. So, instead of a few hours, I devote days on simple tasks.

Two weeks before the ball, Mary invites me over for her final dress fitting. I can hardly spare the time, but I go.

"What do you think?" she asks, turning around several times in front of the mirror so I can absorb the full effect. Her sleeveless white gown is trimmed with delicate lace and ribbon, also white. Elbow-length white silk gloves transform her from a seventeen-year-old girl into a sophisticated young woman.

"Of course, my hair will be up, and curled. And my parents are giving me a gorgeous string of pearls."

"Mary, you look beautiful. Your father will be proud to present you, but . . . "

"But what?"

"But do you really need me there? If it's only because your mother needs more girls, perhaps . . . "

I resist saying something about the stack of work on my desk. Silently, Mary turns around for me to unbutton the back of her dress. Halfway through the buttons, she still hasn't said anything. I sense her disappointment, or is it anger?

True, I'm often baffled by what people expect of me, but at this moment I know perfectly well. I will not spoil her moment by saying another word about my burdens. I will not sacrifice our friendship for good marks.

"Mary, I do have one question for you."

"And that is?" she asks, voice hoarse.

"Should I wear my blue or green gown?"

Mary's smile is all I need to prove I made the right decision.

* * *

On the day of the ball, Mama and Emma spend hours fitting my green gown, and then more hours fussing over my hair. Papa makes a big production of escorting me down our grand staircase and out to the horse-drawn carriage he hired for the occasion. I could walk to the hall, but he insists. I hug him before climbing in.

Any doubts I may have about going melt away with Mary's warm welcome. Watching each father and daughter glory in the spotlight touches me. When it's Mary and Reverend McLean's turn, I note every detail. After all, I did promise to help Mama with Emma's coming out.

The hall erupts into applause as the girls line up on the stage for a last synchronized curtsy, each clutching a pink-and-red floral bouquet. When the band strikes up a waltz, fathers and daughters fill the dance floor. Guilt overwhelms me. Papa would have loved this. Fortunately, he will have Emma as his willing partner.

At three the next morning, with the remnants of the midnight buffet long gone, the orchestra plays its last tune. As I say goodbye, Mary whispers, "You truly *are* my best friend. Thank you."

After a few hours' sleep, I'm back at my desk. To my amazement, I'm able to finish my work on time, including Miss Connors's assignment. I hand her the drawings, twenty in all, each labeled in neat architectural script, and each far more detailed than required.

"Very nice," she says, peering at me over her reading spectacles.

My final grade in her class is also "very nice."

Chapter 17

"WELL DONE, DAUGHTER"

I n January new troubles arrive. Several teachers stay
home with heavy colds. Before long, scores of pupils
take to bed. Mama watches us carefully, me in particular. Her eagle eye doesn't help. I'm the first to fall,
suffering from a violent headache, body aches, and chills.
Fever, weakness, and uncontrollable coughing follows. I'm
sure one rib is cracked. Emma is sick too.

"Warm. We must all stay warm," Mama reports, after
Dr. Wilcox departs. "It's our best protection," she says,
poking the logs in our bedroom fireplace.

Papa stands by the bedroom door. "At least it's not
contagious. Some kind of peculiar atmospheric condition,
he says. He left us some of those quinine tablets. There's
quite a run on them. I'm glad we've got these. Quinine
and a hot bath—a sure cure."

A week later, after my entire family and half of Oakland
suffer with identical symptoms, the doctors change their
minds. We are in the midst of an influenza epidemic, they
declare. Predictably, just when I'm well enough to go back to

school, my ear rebels. I endure the pain silently. Homework assignments accumulate. Graduation and admission to Berkeley depend on work I have not yet begun. Between ear pain and fatigue, I push on.

On top of everything, my violin needs my attention. One day after class, I am asked to join a musical foursome. "Haydn," Phillip Carleton insists. "I like his *String Quartet in C Major*—the perfect choice for graduation. I'll play viola, of course. William and Julia on violin, and John on cello."

I've never played with these three before, but they are known to be the most musically talented in our class. Though I'm familiar with the piece, playing with three others requires considerable practice. Fortunately, graduation is still two months away.

"Can we practice at your house, Julia?" John asks. They eye me closely. They must have heard about Bridget's cookies.

With the uncertainty about my admission to the university, the remainder of the semester is stressful. Finally, after our last exams, Mary and I receive our hoped-for invitations to join the freshman class at the University of California. With high school graduation ceremonies now looming, we barely have time to congratulate each other.

At home, the news is greeted with hugs. During Emma's, she whispers into my ear, "Leave room for me, Dudu. I'm coming too." Instead of a hug from Parm, he presents me with white lilies, traditional for expressing condolences. "Congrats, Sis," he says. "It's your funeral."

The night before our graduation, I sit on Mary's bed, listening to her practice her oration one last time. "Faith and truth, the mightiest of all forces," she concludes, her voice quivering.

"Beautiful, Mary, and so inspiring. I'm sure there won't be a dry eye."

Mary beams. "This is it, you know, Julia. This is truly the moment we leave our childhood behind."

"You said that when we started high school."

"I know," she says, a smile brightening her face. "I'm feeling sentimental."

"Did you ever imagine we'd both be going to college?"

"Never. It's like a dream. Imagine, me studying literature."

"You'll be a wonderful teacher, Mary."

"And you'll be a great engineer," she teases, knowing perfectly well that for me, engineering is a stop along the way to my real dream—architecture.

"And what makes you think I'll be so great?"

"Would I ask you to design a house for me if I didn't?"

For an instant, I envision the house I will create for her—elegant, welcoming, and practical, like my friend.

Three years ago, when I started high school, our class numbered over fifty. Now twenty-eight of us, eighteen boys and ten girls, prepare to march down the aisle of the First Congregational Church to receive our diplomas.

I had never seen the church so beautiful. The second-year class decorated the pulpit with our class colors—pink geraniums against a background of bright green willow branches. They cleverly spell our class motto: *Manners Maketh Man.*

Papa, distinguished in his new top hat, sits on the pulpit with the other school board members. Mary's oration receives thunderous applause. Our string quartet never played better or with more fervor. When we stand for our bow, shouts of "encore" catch me off guard.

Thankfully, Mr. Fish, the board president, tells us to be seated. Still, I'm pleased that the audience wanted to hear more of our music. As he calls us up one-by-one to receive our diplomas, he stands aside for Papa when he comes to my name. Walking to the front, I'm aware of the rustling of petticoats and soft murmurs.

With a slight bow, Papa hands me my diploma, rolled and tied with pink and green ribbons. Despite his solemn face, his eyes sparkle. "Well done, daughter," he says, so only I hear. "Now, make us just as proud at the university."

Returning to my seat, I glance down at the front row. Mama, Grandmother, Parm, Emma, Sam, and Avery are clapping and smiling. Behind them, sitting erect on the edge of her seat, Miss Connors claps longer and harder than anyone. If permitted, I would have done the same for her. Absorbing the moment, I let the goodwill in the hall enfold and lift me—a feeling I know I will draw upon during the next four years. I have a good idea of the challenges ahead.

Part III
The Maze

University Library, Bacon Hall

Chapter 18

SISTERS ALL

Ticking off the days on my calendar does little to speed up the start of college, although a surprise invitation helps. Mary gets one too.

Walking arm in arm to an address near Lake Merritt, Mary complains about her new boots. When we finally spot Mabel Gray's house, I press my lips together. Since I declared my interest in architecture, Mary asserts that I talk too much about those matters. So, I say nothing about how the afternoon sun brightens the expansive patio. I avoid pointing out how the windows offer a breathtaking view of the shimmering lake dotted with sailing boats and swooping gulls.

"I'll never forget our first time here," Mary says, adjusting a straw hat ringed with yellow silk posies.

"Mabel's party?"

"Not just any party—a high school party."

"Mostly I remember being in awe of all those seniors," I say, recalling my shyness.

"Imagine. Today it's all girls . . . college girls!"

The parlor is set up with two rows of chairs. From our seats in the back row I recognize a few girls who graduated high school ahead of us.

Promptly at two o'clock, Mabel calls the meeting to order.

"Welcome, everybody," she says earnestly. "We have a great deal of business ahead, so without further ado, let me introduce Miss Emily Hamilton, a member of Kappa Alpha Theta. It's due to her hard work that we're here today, ready to start Berkeley's own chapter of Kappa Alpha Theta, the first fraternity for girls on campus. I'm certain you're familiar with the boys' fraternities."

Mabel waits for us to finish our giggles. Stories of the high jinks among the fraternity brothers are a popular topic at Oakland High.

Emily stands in front of the room. Stray blond curls escape the bun on top of her head. I admire her neat fitting jacket and skirt, stylish even without fancy buttons and braiding.

"If you think it's difficult being a girl student at Berkeley today, imagine what it was like twenty years ago at DePauw University, where Kappa Alpha Theta started. Today we're asking you to become a member of this special sisterhood. We selected you because you are the cream of the crop, the best and the brightest. Look around this room. Each of you represents the highest academic standing, either at Berkeley or your high school."

I follow the discussion with mild interest, until she introduces a girl sitting in the front row.

"I'd like you to meet Miss Jessie Watson, a new member. Her father has promised to build a house for us."

I pay close attention, especially to the part about the house being finished next fall. I envision myself there, tucked away in my own room, surrounded by my books.

Later, on our walk home, Mary and I chatter like grammar school kids.

"Gee whiz, Julia. Isn't this grand? Starting college with a group of friends, all of us fraternity sisters in Kappa Alpha Theta. But of course, you'll always be my best chuckaboo," she adds, linking her arm through mine.

"Golly, Mary, you haven't started college and you're already talking like one of them. Chuckaboo! Really!"

"Okay, Julia. Spill. What'd you like best?"

"Guess."

"Theta house?"

I grin. "How'd you know?"

"My natural genius," Mary laughs. "I'm guessing you'll want to live there, but what about your parents?"

"We'll see."

Happily, they support my joining Thetas, especially after I explain the invitation is only for top girls. They also see the wisdom of my having an instant circle of friends.

"This is good for you," Mama says, eyebrows furrowed. "If left to your own devices, you'd be studying night and day. At least I can put that worry aside for the next four years."

I omit telling my parents about another benefit. It will only increase their concern about my studying engineering. It was something an older girl said: "The three of us standing here will be seniors. We've learned a thing or two from our experience, especially when it comes to the male students. Not all of them will be happy to see you."

The biggest miracle? My parents agree that when Theta house is finished, I can live there. This will save me two hours a day riding on the trolley. I will be able to walk to class as well as study far from the demands of my dear but distracting family. Naturally, there is a condition. I must keep my promise to our pastor, to teach Sunday school on weekends.

But how can I wait an entire year for this bit of paradise?

In the meantime, Mary pulls a fast one. "I have an announcement, Julia. Drum roll, please."

"Come on. Just tell me."

"The McLeans are moving to Berkeley."

"Berkeley? That is big news."

I want to be happy for Mary, but I feel as if my chuckaboo is abandoning me. I force a smile, even though I already miss her.

"We move before school starts." And then she adds, "I'm really sorry."

"For what?"

Sorry for abandoning me? Sorry for not giving me a warning?

"I'm sorry we won't be riding the trolley together."

I adore Mary, but I don't believe her for a second. She's lucky and she knows it. I console myself, knowing that we will see each other at school.

❋ ❋ ❋

August finally arrives along with the hot weather we hoped for all summer. August also means registration day at the university. Sheffield Sanborn, my chaperone, waits for me at the trolley stop.

Parm was the logical choice for my escort, but his job rules him out. Sheffield and I graduated together from Oakland High School. When Mama learned that he would also be at the university, she prevailed upon his mother for his services.

As expected, Sheff is punctual. Naturally, he's clutching a book. While I'm not known for making brilliant conversation, Sheff makes me seem like a blathering ninny. I've known him for years, and in that time, I never heard him say more than a few words—the ideal chaperone.

"Good Morning, Sheffield."

He tips his hat, always the gentleman. "Morning."

"Excited about our first day?"

"Guess so."

"What will you study?" I ask, dropping my token into the conductor's coin box. Sheff mumbles something, takes a seat, and opens his book. His long legs stretch into the aisle, an instant obstacle.

Two tired horses pull our trolley along the Telegraph Avenue tracks. The trip to campus is so slow I could walk faster than these two old nags.

After the longest thirty minutes of my life, the conductor finally shouts "Temescal Station." The trolley empties as we rush aboard a waiting steam train, its smokestack belching black soot. Thirty minutes later, after a fast, smooth ride, the train pulls into Berkeley Station.

"See you at six," I say to Sheff who is busy buttoning and unbuttoning his jacket.

"Sure thing. Last train of the day. Don't want to miss it," he mumbles before making a hasty departure, disappearing into the crowd with a few long strides.

Chapter 19

A NEW DIGGER

I join the crush of students heading to campus. Ignoring the commotion around me, I stop to inhale the familiar spicy scent of eucalyptus trees and savor the shade of giant oaks. Crossing a footbridge over burbling Strawberry Creek, I leave the trees behind for a well-trodden dirt path meandering through summer-gold grassland.

Boys crowd around me, laughing and joking, many wearing gray or black top hats. I'm familiar with this hat-wearing tradition, thanks to Parmelee.

"Gray plugs for Juniors. Black for Seniors," he instructed. "The more battered and trampled the better. I know it looks silly, but they take the whole thing very seriously."

Without warning, a hatless boy in front of me uses a cane to swipe another boy's gray plug with such ferocity it takes flight. I brace for a fight. Instead, the hat's owner roars with laughter.

"Nice hit, Haverford," the victim shouts good-naturedly. "A few more of those and my hat'll be ready." Parmelee was right. Battered hats are indeed a mark of pride, although he neglected to mention second year students with canes. I suspect there are other customs to learn.

Ahead are two buildings perched on a small rise. South Hall, the four-story brick and stone building, sits on my right. I head left, toward North Hall, four stories of elaborately decorated wood, much like my old high school. Several young men lounge on the steps of two outside staircases.

"Oh, oh. Another pelican invades our hallowed halls," one boy says to a girl walking in front of me.

"Bet that one's a digger," mocks another as I pass. I ignore his wisecrack.

Later I learn they call us pelicans because of our white shirtwaists, which is probably why my Theta sisters prefer blue blouses. The boys reserve the term "diggers" for students with the highest marks. How do they know I plan to live up to this nickname?

Inside the building a line of students snakes down the hallway. I must be in the right place—the recorder's office. I line up behind a tall, skinny boy with a moustache. Every so often, he glances back at me. The closer we get to the front, the more he fidgets.

Finally, he turns around. "Excuse me miss, but Special Students register in the basement, Room 28."

"Thank you," I reply, hiding my irritation. *Special Students* are mostly girls who take a few classes before leaving to marry. If he wanted to insult me, he found the right way.

When I don't budge, he grumbles, "Let me repeat that. SPECIAL STUDENTS DO NOT REGISTER HERE."

"I heard you clearly the first time."

He shrugs his shoulders. "Fine."

When I finally enter the recorder's room, the single line divides into two. The clerk on the left asks the irritating young man his name. "Last name first. First name last."

"Saph. Augustus Valentine Saph. S-A-P-H," he spells out.

"School of entry?"

"Mechanical Engineering."

The clerk on the right asks me the same question. "Name, miss?"

"Morgan. Julia."

"School of entry?"

"Mechanical Engineering."

Several heads turn my way. The recorder's pen freezes in midair.

"Certain about that?" he asks. Pausing, he adds, "An unusual choice for a young lady. Are you sure you don't mean English Literature?"

"Oh, beg your pardon. I didn't mean Mechanical Engineering."

"Ah, I didn't think so." He visibly relaxes then repeats the question. "School of Entry?"

"Civil Engineering would be more accurate. It's within the school of Mechanical Engineering. You may write that any way you please."

I sense Mr. Saph staring.

By the time I finish, he's gone. Not surprisingly, I discover we are in many of the same classes—English, geometry, algebra, trigonometry, and chemistry. My only Saph-free classes are French and lady's archery.

Two weeks after classes begin, I decide to change my seat in chemistry from the back of the room where I sit with the few girls. Moving closer to the front, I foolishly select Mr. Saph's row. As I make my way to an empty seat next to him, he sets his hat on it.

"Taken," he says. The room quiets.

I move two seats away.

"Same for that one," Saph says loudly. "In fact, this whole row is reserved."

"All of it?"

"Let me restate that." He surveys the room, pretending to search for another empty seat before saying, "I've found a perfectly fine seat for you, Miss Morgan. At home with your mother. Your duties there are far more important than taking up some gentleman's seat at college."

The men roar their approval, stamping their feet. Saph grins. They're all watching. My first test. Raising my chin, I deliberately move to the seat next to Saph, hand him his hat, and sit.

"Hey Saph, got a new girlfriend?" hoots a boy a few rows back.

There are more guffaws.

Pretending to ignore their vulgar behavior, I pull a notebook and pen from my satchel. Folding my damp hands on the desk, I feign calm, praying for the professor's arrival.

I think about the teasing I endured in high school. I think about how Parmelee tormented me. At that instant I'm almost grateful for those years of preparation.

Chapter 20

TOUGH START

By seven thirty in the morning, I'm standing at the trolley stop with good old reliable Sheff. When I found out he was studying ancient history, Greek and Latin, and classical literature, our entire conversation changed.

"Good morning, Sheffield."

"Good morning, Julia."

"Lots of homework?"

"You bet."

"Well, Rome wasn't built in a day you know."

Grinning, he walks to his usual seat and opens a book. Apparently, he appreciates my little joke about ancient Rome. His smile lingers for several blocks.

Whenever possible, Mary and I share a hurried lunch. We meet in a special place reserved for women students called The Ladies' Room. I cherish this dark, private space—long and narrow, running the full length of North Hall's basement.

The seven hundred men on campus have their pick of gentlemen-only clubs, social activities, athletic fields, and private benches. The Ladies' Room is the only place for us co-eds. Here we study and relax on comfy chairs and couches. We can store our overcoats, books, and such in lockers. And we can eat lunch and complain to our hearts' content. When the cold months arrive, we push the couches and chairs closer to the coal-heated potbelly stove. This is our sanctuary away from the men's disapproving looks and daily slights. No matter how early I arrive, a potbelly stove warms the room.

After winter break, Mary and I catch up over a shared bologna sandwich. Curled up on the couch closest to the heat, she explains the magic of the always-toasty fire. "We have Jimmie Tait to thank."

"Who's Jimmie Tait?"

"You've seen him, haven't you, Julia? The famous janitor of North Hall?"

"I'm not sure."

"Dark hair? Cap? Feather duster at his side? He's everywhere. Dusting, cleaning, and of course, he's our bell ringer. Who do you think rings that bell at the end of classes?"

"And makes sure we have enough coal too. You're right, Mary. How would we manage without him?"

I'm especially grateful to Jimmie Tait when March blows in, along with its wet, windy, wild weather. None of us walk outside without our overshoes. I become adept at avoiding mud puddles on my trek between buildings, thanks to a few well-positioned boards set over the deepest puddles.

* * *

One gray, stormy day as I race from chemistry in South Hall to French in North Hall, I stumble. I have never before lost my footing on the planks, but a scuffed-up boot cunningly placed in my path does its worst. Sitting in the muck and mud, books and papers scattered everywhere, I hear the laughter. When I finally look up, everyone has mysteriously vanished. I pull my hand from the thick, sticky muck. Unwittingly, I wipe strands of loose hair from my eyes. Now mud decorates both my face *and* clothes. At the same moment, black clouds break open, releasing buckets of rain.

I cannot go to French class like this. Gathering my things, I head for the Ladies' Room. As soon as I open the door, expressions of sympathy greet me like a warm blanket.

Oh no!

What happened to you?

You poor thing.

A circle of sympathetic girls surrounds me, Mary among them. One pries muddy books from my arms. Another liberates my umbrella from a clenched fist.

Mary guides me to the glowing potbelly stove, then barks orders, "Add more coal." Then "Water. Rags. Find Jimmie Tait."

By the time Jimmie Tait delivers a bowl of warm water and a towel, I'm settled in the rocking chair by the fire clutching a cup of hot tea, warmed by a blanket across my shoulders. My outrage fades. Watching as the girls dab my mud-spattered skirt with damp towels, I regain my composure until it hits me.

"My French class! I'm sure to be docked," I moan.

"It'd be far worse if you came into class like this," Mary says, gently blotting a mud stain on my jacket sleeve.

"But it's my day for recitation."

The room quiets. Missing recitation is a serious breach. Most of the girls detest standing in front of the class quizzed by the professor. While I don't mind, Professor Paget is a stickler. Muddy clothes are no excuse.

As the rain continues throughout the day, I fret over missing class. The girls convince me that the men's ridicule would be worse than missing French recitation. By six o'clock I head to the train with other students, guided by boys who light our way with lanterns. I'm almost presentable, though missing French still troubles me.

Aboard the train, I wonder if Sheff will notice my state of disrepair. Naturally, he does not. But after a few minutes he closes his book to ask me a surprising question.

"You're in a fraternity, aren't you?"

"I am."

"Did you know I joined one, too?"

I'm shocked. During all these months, I thought of Sheff as a quiet, studious loner.

"Which house?"

"Beta Theta Pi. The Betas. I hear you're a Theta."

"That's right. It's new. In fact, we don't have a building yet. But when it's finished our trolley days will be over. I'm moving in."

He sits up, pulling his oversized feet from the aisle. "Well, that's good. I'm moving into my house, too. Next year. The fellows are great. I can't wait."

What is happening to Sheff? He said more in the last minute than the entire year.

Then, snap! He's back to normal, vanishing into his book. Across the aisle, a group of upperclassmen jabber about the latest campus prank, apparently the work of my fellow freshmen.

The Chinaman's laundry cart. That's what Fitch told me they used.

Stealing the cart was easy.

Their laughter fills the trolley. I have seen the Chinese man with his cart, picking up soiled clothes from boarding houses and fraternities, then returning them, clean and folded. Back and forth, back and forth, never stopping. I'm certain he isn't laughing. I picture his filled laundry bag casually tossed aside.

Yeah, but then they got stuck.

Couldn't get the cart onto Harmon Gym's roof.

There must have been twenty of them in on the prank.

Had to leave the cart on the ground, a bit battered.

More laughter.

The poor man's livelihood depends on his cart. A cruel act, but not surprising. Every day the newspaper describes such incidents. Only yesterday I read about a group of drunken hoodlums who beat up a Chinese man for no reason. "It was fun," they said.

There is nothing funny about this hateful prank. I'm tempted to say something to the boys but know that will only encourage their ridicule. Instead, I imagine telling off the bullies who stole the cart. Had they possessed a simple knowledge of physics and pully systems, one scrawny boy could have pulled that cart up to the roof. I do not intend to share this secret with them.

❋ ❋ ❋

The next day I stand before a scowling Professor Paget.

"I'm sorry, Miss Morgan. Rules are rules. No rescheduling of recitations. Perhaps next time you'll be here." I watch him scribble a large, red *F* in his grade book next to all the high marks I've already earned.

Not surprisingly, everything is different for the boys. How many times did I watch them apologize for missing a recitation because the trolley came off the tracks? How many times have I observed them deliberately rock the trolley until it left the tracks so they would have a *legitimate* excuse for being late? How many times did Professor Paget accept their silly story? How unfair.

My Theta sisters face the same treatment in their classrooms, which is why our weekly fraternity meeting starts with airing the daily slights and offenses we all endure.

Until Theta House is ready, we meet at the home of Professor and Mrs. Bernard Moses. She was a Theta years ago at another university. Though quiet at our meetings, she listens attentively. My run-in with Professor Paget, however, moves her to speak.

"How unfortunate," she murmurs. "I didn't think that happened any longer."

Dorothy, who also tends to be quiet, raises her hand. "It's worse than ever, Mrs. Moses. I've never told this to anyone. When it happened to me, I didn't know what to do."

There are nods of encouragement. Dorothy continues. "I'm an English major. Teaching is what I want to do more than anything. I've a few required classes left, one in American literature."

Mary leans forward in her chair.

"On the first day of school I tried to enroll in Professor Lange's class, but he turned me away, saying it was full. I knew that wasn't true, but I didn't argue. What could I say?"

"You should have told him that's not right," Mabel breaks in. "We have to stand up."

Dorothy shakes her head. "And what good would that do? I learned that Professor Lange shuts the door on lots of girls. He doesn't think we belong here. He's fond of saying that we are better suited for baking than books."

The girl's voices rise like a swarm of angry bees.

When the buzz fades, Dorothy says, "I found another class, nearly as good."

"Still, we must do something," says our vice president, Lulu Heacock. "Each of us has felt invisible, or judged, or examined under the men's microscope. It's not right."

Here she stops, slowly looking around the room. "We must do something, say something. And we shall."

Heads nod. Everyone sits straighter.

I so admire her grit. She's tough and strong.

"This is why we start our meetings on this subject. Look around the room, my friends. Everyone here has experienced painful moments like this. We are here for you, always."

The room is silent. Lulu turns towards me. "Julia? Do you have a report for us?"

Because of my interest in architecture, my job is to keep the girls up to date on the construction of Theta House. I love the work, spending far more time on it than necessary, but I cannot help it. There are drawings to create and an endless list of decisions to check off.

"Yes, Lulu. I do. We need to make an important

decision," I alert them. "As you know, we're on schedule to move into our house by the end of summer."

Frowns turn to smiles.

"At our last meeting, you all thought we should paint our new house pale blue with white trim for the house. Is that right?"

A chorus of *yes* fills the room. I do not agree with this choice, but I know how to change their minds. I pull two drawings from my briefcase. Holding up one, I say, "This is how the house would look if we paint the body blue and all the trim white—the columns, window frames, and wood ornaments."

Mary speaks first. "It's lovely, Julia. It'll be the prettiest house on the block."

"I know you like it, but in my opinion, these colors make the house look dead."

They burst into laughter. Mabel raises her hand. "Dead? Why, Julia, how can a house look dead?"

"I'll show you."

I hold up a second drawing. The room quiets. On this one I used a different set of colors. The body of the house is dark tan. The pillars, trim, and window frames are a light cream, and a narrow band of dark brown highlights the window sashes. "Do you see how the boldness of the dark brown enlivens those beige and tan colors? Now compare this image to the blue and white version. Do you see how the house disappears?"

I hold up the two drawings, side-by-side. "Take your time. Which house does the best job of telling the world that the women of Kappa Alpha Theta live here?" When the vote is called, all hands are raised for my colors.

* * *

That April, Grandmother passes away, quietly in her sleep.
I have been expecting this. She has been sleeping more
and eating less, but when it happens, I'm heartsick. Mama
weeps for days.

Mama, Papa, and Parmelee decide to accompany the
coffin to Brooklyn for her burial beside Grandfather's
grave. I want to go, to honor my grandmother. And the
trip would allow me to visit with Cousin Pierre. His skyscraper is finally going up. Letters, though infrequent, tell
about his trials and tribulations.

> *No more designing churches and firehouses for*
> *me. From now on, I'm building straight up. The*
> *Metropolitan Life Building is going to put my*
> *name on the map. The foundation pilings are*
> *in, but as I wrote earlier, the work is plagued by*
> *too much ground water. I'm using pumps. My*
> *engineer feels certain there cannot be much water*
> *left. I hope he is right.*

Architects and engineers often work together especially
when designing a skyscraper. I long to see the outcome.
Unfortunately, a trip east would take five days on the
train each way, plus a week for the funeral activities. With
exams around the corner, sadly such a trip is impossible.

A few weeks later, when exams are finished, I pick
up my grades at North Hall. Scanning my grade report,
I'm satisfied. Good grades in all subjects, even French
and English.

"Miss Morgan. Is that a smile on your usually dour face?"

I look up. Saph is eyeing me, a single eyebrow arched. Silently, I fold the report into a small square before slipping it into my pocket.

"You don't have to say a word. It's well known that you're a first-class digger. But don't worry. I relish competition," he adds, tipping his hat. At that moment the man nicknamed "The Angel of Death," arrives. The hall turns as quiet as a tomb. His presence means one thing—those notes he is about to post on the board contain news of students with failing grades, which explains so many pale faces hovering nearby.

Saph snickers, and then in a voice that echoes down the corridor, he booms, "*Doomsday is near; die all, die merrily.*" Pausing to make sure I'm watching, he continues. "That's Shakespeare, Miss Morgan. Something you might possibly recognize from English class."

With a spine-tingling laugh, he exits, tipping his hat to The Angel of Death.

Chapter 21

MY LIFE CHANGES

Summer vacation means solitary walks on shaded trails, putting up jars of blackberry preserves with Mama and Bridget, and a week to explore Santa Cruz's beaches. Least enjoyable is accompanying Mama on her tiresome social calls when Emma cannot.

Time and again the ladies ask, "Tell us, Julia, how is college life?"

I struggle to find a satisfactory answer. Lately, I rely on a vague but acceptable answer: "It has its challenges, but nothing I can't handle." Occasionally I add, "And the girls in my fraternity are wonderful." I omit telling them what I love most. I leave out how solving mathematical problems is like solving a tantalizing puzzle, fitting each piece together leading to a satisfying solution. I am silent about the mystery and magic of chemistry.

Before classes resume, two events change my life—one helpful and one noteworthy. The first is the opening of the electric road with its trolley. Suddenly the time it takes for me to travel from home to campus is cut in half. The noteworthy event? The opening of Theta House.

In late August, I take Sam for his first trolley ride on the electric road. The tired horses who pulled those trolleys around town have been retired to their stables. Excitement over this modern mode of transportation runs high. Red, white, and blue flags and banners flutter from the porches lining Telegraph Avenue, the trolley's main route. People crowd street corners to watch the show. As the trolley rolls by, electrical wires flash overhead, sparking and crackling like the Fourth of July.

"These trolleys look a lot like a San Francisco cable car," Sam observes as he drops his nickel in the coin box. If not for the metal rod connecting to the electric lines overhead, Sam would be right. The trolley is an exact replica of those cable cars. He follows me to the open-air benches in the rear.

Dropping my bundle to the floor, Sam complains. "Golly, Dudu. I'd rather carry your books than this thing. Have you put iron bars inside?"

Tapping the bundle with my toe, I give him a hint. "The ingredients for my latest beautification project. Top secret work for Theta House. We're ready for move-in. You'll see soon enough."

The sack includes everything I need to reupholster a well-used couch: a hammer, a tape measure, tacks, scissors, and floral fabric—pale yellow chintz splashed with red and pink zinnias.

"This is the right job for you," Mary assured me when I expressed doubts about my abilities. "You're careful, a good planner, and thorough."

Our new Theta House is abuzz with activity. From my workplace near the parlor window, I can watch the girls bustling around in their headscarves and aprons, cleaning floors, ceilings, and anything else that doesn't move. The workmen left wood shavings in every nook and cranny. Everyone pitches in.

Meanwhile, I work on the couch. My diligence makes me the butt of good-natured teasing. I'm quickly learning how such teasing is part of living with whip-smart girls with a sense of humor.

My goodness, Julia, I didn't think one little couch could take so many tacks.

That piece of furniture is likely to last longer than any of us.

Who would have guessed that tacks could make such a beautiful design? I've never seen anything like it. Never!

Mary and I stand in front of my finished couch, her arm resting on my shoulder. "You see. I was right. No one else could have done the job as well."

After the sofa project, I pitch in washing windows and planting flowers along the pathway to the front door. I'm surprised how much I enjoy completing these chores with the girls.

On move-in day, Mama, Papa, and Sam are at Theta house to meet the delivery wagon. The men trudge upstairs with my trunk, bed, desk, chairs, full-length mirror, and chest of drawers. Standing in the middle of my room, Mama directs Sam and Papa on where to place everything. They have such a good time I stay silent, knowing that when they leave, I shall move the furniture to where I like.

Downstairs, Mama corners Mrs. Lee, the stern lady

we hired as our housemother. Curious, I sidle up to a cookie tray nearby, lingering over my selection.

"And how do you plan to do everything? This is a big job," Mama asks. I wince. Mama has difficulty not being in charge.

Mrs. Lee is unruffled. "Oh, I've done this before, Mrs. Morgan. I know how to find good help. There's no lack of eager students needing money. Nothing to it."

By the time the interview ends, both women exchange thin smiles.

Our new cook, Smithy, also earns high marks. The test? Not a single cookie is left on the trays.

After our families leave, Lulu Heacock, our newly elected president, assembles us in the front parlor. I know her brother Harry from Oakland High. She looks like him. Tall, blond, and the same freckles splayed across her nose. The seniors take their places on the couches. The rest of us sit on the floor, something we never do at home.

"Well, Thetas," she begins. "Look around you. Isn't this grand?"

We applaud enthusiastically.

"But we can't rest. Our calendar is chockablock full, and we need everyone's help."

As Lulu describes what awaits us, I clench my hands. Classes have not yet started, and I already feel the pull between schoolwork and the Theta calendar.

"Everyone has a job, but let me be frank. With only three of our seven bedrooms filled, we're already running short of money. Please think about moving into our beautiful new house. That would be a big help."

Lulu's hankie is getting a workout. The usual September heat leaves us dripping. Still, she carries on. "Next Monday will be our first lunch here, and every day thereafter. No more Ladies' Room."

I cheer with the others.

At Monday's lunch, everyone's excited chatter makes it difficult to hear. I itch to retreat to my room where calculus and physics assignments wait, but I restrain myself. After all, this is only the first day of classes.

* * *

A new torment awaits me on campus. Several of my classes are located in the Mechanical Arts Building. Its ground floor is jam-packed with machinery, models, laboratories, and male students. As soon as I open the front door, the place turns eerily quiet. The machines stop. I pass a gauntlet of disapproving stares. The chatter only resumes when I reach the staircase.

By the time I reach my desk upstairs, I face more disapproving stares. But when class begins, I am transfixed by the work, sketching from memory any tool or machine in precise detail, the form and dimensions exact to the smallest part of an inch. If not for Mr. Augustus Valentine Saph's frequent glances at my drawings, this would be a most satisfying experience.

During lunch at Theta House, I seek Mary's opinion. "Saph baffles me," I admit, nibbling one of Smithy's homemade rolls.

"Maybe he's surprised a girl can draw so well."

"Maybe."

"But Julia, this explains everything."

"What?"

"Why you always beat me at archery."

"I *am* excellent at archery, aren't I?"

"Indeed."

"But what does that have to do with Mr. Saph's endless staring at my work?"

"It's simple. You have this remarkable ability. You know precisely how to hit the bullseye. It's uncanny. But that's not all. Remember when we mounted all those wall hangings on move-in day, and we asked for your advice on where to hammer the nails?"

"Yes."

"That's because you see things we don't, like distance and height. It's like you have a level in your brain. You can also see if something is tipped the smallest amount. I think Mr. Saph cannot believe his eyes."

Her words ring true. I can tell the precise distance of objects. Once I have a particular number in my brain, I never forget it. And yes, I can see tilts and uneven spaces. I thought everyone saw the world this way, but maybe not, and probably not Mr. Saph.

Chapter 22

GOWNS & FUR

Last year I skipped the Freshman Hop, the big dance at Harmon Gymnasium. "Schoolwork first" was my motto. This year, while that's still my motto, I resolve to attend the Sophomore Hop, partly because I'm unwilling to face another round of badgering from my Theta sisters. They hounded me relentlessly.

Julia, you've got to go. Everyone does.

Where's your class spirit?

One night away from your books won't make that much difference.

My brother's going to be there. You've got to meet him.

There's a second reason I decided to go, something Miss Connors said to me at graduation. "Miss Morgan. I have no doubt you will succeed in your studies. But there is more to college, you know. Other benefits are equally important."

I pretended to understand, but in truth, I couldn't imagine what she meant. Now, after finishing my first year I think I know.

The weekend before the dance, Mama and Emma help select my frock. Ever since her coming-out party, Emma has become mother's confidante for everything social. Instead of a debutante ball, Mama hosted an afternoon tea for Emma, a new way parents present their daughters to society. Flowers filled every nook and cranny our house, along with a profusion of young men, and a steady stream of visitors. The tea went on for hours. Papa looked so proud and Mama so beautiful. And Emma? Well, she glowed, as I knew she would. True to my word, I took part in every decision, attended the gown fittings, and even dived into endless discussions about refreshments without a peep of protest.

Now Mama and Emma fuss over me. Hearing the commotion in my bedroom, Papa cannot stay away.

"You'll be the belle of the ball," he says in high spirits as he watches me model a yellow gown. Avery and Sam stand behind him, craning their neck for a peek.

"Scat," I scold. "Shoo. Away. All of you."

Ignoring me, they laugh until Emma finally closes the door on them.

Ultimately, I agree to a light burgundy gown, comfortable, and more like what I expect the other girls to wear.

On the night of the dance, all the sophomore girls gather in my second-floor bedroom, our temporary "dressing room." Gowns, undergarments, and hairbrushes are scattered everywhere. Girls jostle for a place in front of the mirror.

Please. Someone. Tie my corset.

Ouch. Too tight. Loosen it or I won't be able to eat a thing.

I can't button the back. Help!

The gym is barely recognizable. Instead of the usual climbing equipment, bright lavender-colored flags decorate the hall. Our class of 1894 will certainly be remembered for our strange class color named *heliotrope*. Boughs of evergreens are tucked between the flags, enough to fill a forest. As the orchestra tunes up, there is a stir of anticipation.

In minutes, the dance card dangling from my wrist is filled with boys' names. Surprisingly, first on the list is Sheff. This dance is always a schottische, demanding and lively. Sheff does surprisingly well with the complicated steps. Still, as we spin around the room, I can hear him muttering, "One, two, three, hop. One, two, three, hop." His long legs challenge my shorter ones. He's so busy with the count that conversation is impossible, which is fine with me. I keep up but am relieved when the music ends. Thanking him for the dance, I limp to the punch bowl with only slightly trampled toes.

On my way, I pass a gang of engineering students, Saph in the middle. Thomas Taylor, Saph's annoying sidekick, is there, too. He glowers at me, then says something that makes them laugh.

Hours later, my feet throbbing from the assault of clumsy young men, the master of ceremonies announces the last dance of the evening. I'm glad to see the final name on my dance card is Ben Weed.

I met Ben last month on a Theta hike in the hills above campus. He and a group of sophomore men were guarding a huge boulder they had painted with our school colors—blue and gold—along with a gigantic '94, the year of our class's graduation. Paint spattered their trousers and hands.

Tonight, I barely recognize him in his carefully pressed suit, snappy bow tie, and neatly combed hair. "I thought you might still be up in those hills, guarding your boulder," I tease, as we take our place on the dance floor.

"My boulder's fine. I keep an eye on it."

As we spin around the room, I'm grateful for those dance lessons Mama insisted upon. The last number, always a waltz, is my favorite because of the violins.

"Tell you what, Julia," Ben says, expertly maneuvering us around a cluster of heliotrope flags. "I grew up in Berkeley. I know those hills like the back of my hand. Someday I'll take you to my favorite spot."

With the orchestra's last note, Ben bows. I curtsy. Loosening his tie, he says, "And thus ends my duty as a member of the Sophomore Hop arrangements committee. And you, Miss Morgan, made the job worth the effort."

Later, as I ease into bed, careful of my smashed toes, I realize the girls were right. The Hop wasn't so bad after all. Not all the men at college are like my engineering classmates. I vow to remember this when I see those obnoxious gents act up again. This evening I met some nice boys, clever and interesting. Could this be what Miss Connors meant by those "other" college benefits?

The next day life resumes as usual. Eat. Attend class. Read. Study. Eat. Study. Sleep is last on my list, and never enough. To stay alert in the wee hours, I keep the window wide open and a glass of milk and one of Smithy's chocolate cookies on my desk.

One cold, rainy night, while deep into calculus, I'm distracted by a tiny sound. Tearing myself away from a confounding problem, I look up. Sitting on my windowsill is a dainty black-and-white cat. Its bright green eyes are staring at me. I'm startled but wise enough to remain still.

"Hello, little thing. How'd you get up here?"

The cat mews a reply. Water drips from the tips of her ears.

"Wet out there, is it?"

Still staring at me, she licks a white paw.

"Want to come in? Here. Have some milk."

I pour the rest of my milk into the saucer, nudging the dish toward her. She hesitates, but not for long.

When the saucer is licked clean, I have a new dilemma. I cannot imagine shooing her back outside into the storm nor can I imagine inviting her to stay. Reaching out my hand, she steps close enough to allow a scratch under her chin and behind her ears. Will she stay or leave? It doesn't take long to find out. Leaping from my desk to the floor, she circles the room then springs onto the rocker, and onto cozy afghan invitingly arranged on its seat.

"You've made yourself at home, haven't you?"

Purring, she curls into a ball, tucks in her tail, and closes her eyes.

The rocker is empty in the morning. While I am disappointed, I decide it's for the best. I certainly don't need a cat, and neither do the Thetas.

Still, she returns the next night, laps up her milk, makes a beeline for the rocker, and is asleep by the time I crawl into bed. And so, the routine continues with one difference. Now she lets me hold and stroke her before going to her blanket.

I keep my night visitor secret until one day at lunch, when I tap my glass with a spoon. "Announcement," I say.

The room quiets.

"I have a new friend, someone I'd like you to meet. She's shy, but once she gets to know you, she's quite friendly."

"A new friend? Why Julia, do invite her to lunch," Lulu says, always urging us to bring guests to Theta House.

"She has four dainty white paws, soft black-and-white fur, the longest tail, and the greenest eyes you've ever seen on a cat."

I was surprised by the hilarity that followed my announcement. Within days, the girls decide on a name for our midnight visitor. Lulu makes the announcement. "Henceforth we shall call her Kat. Isn't that perfect? That's our fraternity's nickname. A fine fit, I think."

Most nights Kat sleeps in my room but occasionally she'll find her way to other bedrooms. Then one night her visits stop. No little Kat. The girls keep asking for her, as does Smithy, who likes having a good mouser in the house.

Just when I lose all hope of ever seeing her again, Kat appears at the usual time on my windowsill with a black, furry, and wiggly something clutched in her mouth. *Please don't be a mouse*, I pray. Kat jumps from my desk to her afghan where she deposits a tiny, mewing kitten, eyes still closed. Before I can admire the pretty little thing, Kat is gone. Minutes later she's back with another squeaky bundle, and another, and another. Four tiny black-and-white kittens cuddle together. Meanwhile, Kat plays the proud mama, licking her tail with exaggerated care.

All the girls fall in love with the kittens. We tell them apart them by their white markings. Before we know it, they're old enough to climb out of their box by themselves.

Now we have new problem—finding homes for the little dears. My biggest surprise? Mama takes one!

"I've always loved cats, Dudu. Why, you remember Dianora Delia and little Foxy don't you?"

"Of course. They were always the first thing I looked for in Grandmother's home."

"Well, I've been thinking it's time we have a cat. One of these is as good as another."

I'm glad Mama picked the tiniest one, my favorite. We call him The Professor because of how his white markings look like a moustache.

Kat claims permanent residency in Theta House where she helps Smithy with the mouse problem and visits me nightly for her saucer of milk. I had not realized the calming effect of a purring cat's warm, furry body. With Kat in my lap, I cannot help wondering if she's another of those "benefits" Miss Conners had in mind.

Chapter 23

SWEET & SOUR

While I may have had doubts about going to the Sophomore Hop, I would never miss a Theta tea. Just before winter vacation we host a tea to honor our friend and booster, Mrs. Moses.

Since guests are welcome, I invite my new chum, Jessica Peixotto. We met in my political economy class taught by none other than Professor Moses. Eight years older than me, I'm drawn to Jessica's maturity and brilliance. Although she started college later than most, she works harder than anyone I know. Every few days we meet at The Ladies' Room, sharing class notes and grievances. We agree on most things, including the belief that women can indeed find happiness outside the home.

Jessica wears an expertly tailored jacket and skirt to the tea, a green gemstone brooch at her neck highlighting her sky-blue eyes. On her way out, she links her arm through mine. "Thank you for inviting me, Julia. I adore this house, and your Theta sisters are first rate."

"I'm glad you came, Jessica."

"Jessie."

"Jessie," I say, feeling as if I have known her forever. "See you in the new year."

"Until next year, Julia. Imagine. 1892 is almost upon us!"

A few months later there is a second tea in which we become the guests of Mrs. Phoebe Hearst. The tea is at an unusual location—Professor LeConte's home, a pleasant walk from Theta House through the Berkeley hills.

On the way, Mary goes on about Mrs. Hearst. I'm familiar with her name, but not much more. "She's quite important, Julia," Mary says, breathless from walking uphill. "She cares about the college, especially the girls. A splendid lady, I've been told."

"I'm glad to hear that Mary, but what about Professor LeConte's home? They say it's one of the nicest in Berkeley."

"It would have to be for Mrs. Hearst to host a tea there."

"Is it true she has an apartment in San Francisco?" I ask, slowing down so the others can catch up.

"An apartment *and* a country home, but Mother's heard she plans to build a house in Berkeley."

Eliza Blake, a new Theta sister, tugs Mary's sleeve. "And what about Mr. Hearst? Wasn't he a senator?"

Dimple-cheeked Annie Brewer squeezes in. "He was. Very rich. Very important, but he died in office."

All of this is news to me. If I would read the newspaper gossip columns or listen to Mama and Emma's chatter about who's who and what's what, I might know about such matters.

Annie rests an arm over Eliza's shoulders. "And don't forget the Hearst's son, William Randolph Hearst. I've seen his picture in the papers. Oh, he's so handsome. Twenty-nine, and already famous."

Though winded by our climb, we squeeze out a laugh.

"Well, he had help," Mary says, stopping to rest. "His father gave him his own newspaper when he was a mere tyke of twenty-four. Imagine owning the *San Francisco Examiner* at that young age."

My thoughts swing to Parmelee, who is nothing like young Mr. Hearst. At twenty-two, my brother still lives at home. Recently he was promoted to bookkeeper at the door company where he works. Since then, Papa has not complained about his eldest son. Still, Parm goes out every night to the beer halls with his friends. He comes home late, sleeps in, and doesn't give a thought to the future.

At the tea, I realize Mrs. Hearst and I have something in common. We see eye to eye—literally. I had given up any hope of reaching five feet, and obviously, so has Mrs. Hearst. Still, she fills the room with her presence!

"So nice to meet you, Miss Morgan," she says, her blue eyes scrutinizing me as I stand in front of the great lady. Later I watch her speak to each of the girls—curious, friendly, and always giving each of us her undivided attention.

Near the end of the tea, Mrs. Hearst gathers us together. "I've enjoyed my afternoon with you ladies. Thank you for coming."

She speaks of her interest in the university and finishes by inviting us to a musical performance. "We're raising money for sports equipment for the women on campus."

There are murmurs of approval. Mabel speaks up. "A capital idea, Mrs. Hearst. We shall certainly attend."

Heads nod.

Mabel is keen on the subject. "It's been such a trial, trying to convince the administration that exercise is good for us. We want tennis and boating. And we want a gymnasium just for girls. While it's true there aren't many of us here, everyday our numbers grow. They need to know we won't give up easily."

As spring approaches, I study nonstop. When not in class, I'm either in my fraternity bedroom or Bacon Hall's library hideaway. Whenever I enter this castle-like tower, I stand for a moment in the middle of the ground floor. From here I can see the two levels above me, their circular floors with decorative curved iron railings. Bookcases on each floor form narrow corridors, like the spokes of a bicycle wheel ending at ceiling-high windows. There, by one of the windows on the second floor, a desk and chair make for a cozy study alcove.

One Friday after returning to my alcove after a short break, an unfamiliar book mysteriously appears on top of my pile.

Women's Suffrage: The Reform Against Nature
By Horace Bushnell

This horrid book, popular on campus, declares that men are more capable than women, especially when it comes to voting and running for office. "Far too great a burden for the *fairer sex*," Bushnell argues. Whoever left the book here also left a note.

Educating women is the thief of time.

I have heard this before. *Women don't belong at the university.* We're *wasting everyone's time*—our own, our professors, even our fellow students.

A muffled sneeze draws my attention to the bookcase in front of me. I spot a pair of eyes gleaming through a narrow space near the top. They blink once then vanish. The owner is Mr. Saph's height.

Turning the offensive book face down, my thoughts are spinning. *Poor Mr. Saph. We have a surprise for you, and you won't like it one bit. Someday, women* will *be able to vote. I promise you. And when that day comes, your horrible book will join the others like it . . . in the trash bin.*

Hours later, still fuming, I pack a small satchel for my weekend at home. Nearing the Berkeley depot, I spot Papa pacing on the platform, his usual chipper smile missing.

I catch a whiff of cigar smoke clinging to his clothes. We have met at the depot before, usually when he has business in Berkeley. "It's Emma," he confides as the train picks up speed. "Your mother's worried."

"Why, what's wrong?"

"Weak heart. Dr. Wilcox says it's a heart murmur."

I'm confused. Emma is the healthiest of us all. A sickly heart could not be more unlikely. Still, I have noticed her sleeping more than usual. There have been occasional complaints of dizziness, typical for excitable, corseted eighteen-year-olds.

"Frankly, Dudu, his theory about her heart is preposterous. Something to do with when you girls had scarlet fever."

How could an illness we had twelve years ago affect us now? I think back on those long months in bed and the doctor's dreaded daily visit. And the waiting for him to say those words that would release us from our prison of pillows. But the doctor did warn us. "Stay in bed. No walking. The slightest exertion could damage your hearts." Under Mama's watchful eye we obeyed every rule. Apparently, our precautions failed to protect Emma's heart or my poor ear.

"Talk to Emma for us," he says. "Naturally, we're not letting her start college next fall. She'll probably be devastated."

As we make our way to Oakland, I try to imagine what Emma will do with her year at home. For me, this would be the worst conceivable fate. I prepare myself for a difficult conversation.

"Oh, Dudu. Don't tell Papa or Mama, but I couldn't be happier," she crows.

"Happy? About not starting college? You must truly be ill, sister. Is there anything I can do for you?"

Emma laughs. "I'm fine, really! I have plans."

"Plans?"

"Yes indeed. Well, one plan. His name is Hart Wyatt North." Her eyes brighten when she says his name.

She met Hart at her coming-out tea, and since then his name is the most overused word in our household. He was ahead of me in high school and went right on to law school like most young men with ambition. I look closely at my sister. Her cheeks are rosy, and her eyes shine. My diagnosis? The silly thing is lovesick.

Chapter 24

TIME OUT FOR FOOLISHNESS

From the start of junior year, I feel as if I'm in a race I cannot possibly win. Not surprisingly, the men in my class are more concerned about their gray plugs. Hats fly everywhere, swatted around by the second-year men with canes. Soon, they are battered and crushed to perfection. This year a few spirited girls wear plugs too. I like their gumption but don't understand why they want to copy these foolish men.

By now I'm accustomed to the tug-of-war between Theta activities, coursework, and weekends at home teaching bible school. I could handle it all, if not for Professor Soulé's engineering course. Everyone calls him "The Colonel," and for good reason. He was a colonel in the army and still prefers standing with hands clasped behind his back, chin slightly raised.

He reserves a special displeasure for me. "Miss Morgan," he barks in class, always taking me by surprise. I stand, steeling myself for his barrage of questions. He rarely lets me finish, inevitably interrupting with, "That will do. You may be seated." I'm certain he grades me harsher than the men. Naturally, this provokes me to work harder.

One afternoon while cramming for yet another of Professor Soulé's tough exams, Jessie Peixotto finds me in my library alcove. "Oh, Julia. I was hoping you'd be here," she whispers, glancing at my pile of books.

Though pleased to see my friend, I keep my finger on the illustration I was studying.

"We need to talk about the Junior Farce."

I'm familiar with this dramatic form, having attended several such plays in church and high school. The plots are always silly, highly improbable, and the characters are ridiculous. Our college tradition is for the junior class to create and perform such a spectacle, an evening I intend to miss.

"You *are* going, aren't you?" Jessie searches my face.

"Are *you*? Why, it's so foolish," I whisper back. Jessie doesn't reply. I say it again. "You agree, don't you?"

"Actually Julia, under normal circumstances, I would. But believe me when I say these are *not* normal circumstances."

I put my textbook down, place my pen in the ink holder, and fold my hands on the tabletop. "Tell me about it."

"You know Frank Norris, don't you?"

"Indeed, I do."

Frank is one of the brightest stars in our class, extremely handsome, with a taste for unconventional clothes. His moustache would leave Parmelee weak with envy. He writes for the school newspaper, and the boy is a popular topic at Theta lunches.

Jessie pushes her chair closer to mine. "I've known Frank for years. He and my brother Ernest are chums. They both like to draw. In fact, they studied drawing together in Paris. It's because of Frank that I'm even here. He's the one who convinced my father to let me enroll."

What could Jessie's relationship with Frank have to do with the Junior Farce? Seeing the confusion on my face she hurries on. "When good friends need you, you help out. Don't you agree?"

"Why, yes. I would like to think so."

"Frank needs me."

I nod, hoping to hurry her along. Professor Soulé's class starts in less than an hour. I was counting on a few more minutes to study the illustration and complete a calculation.

Jessie sighs. "Promise me one thing. When I tell you, you won't laugh?"

"Promise," I whisper back.

"Frank wrote the script for the farce. He's also the director. It's exceedingly silly, as it should be. Slapstick and goofy, naturally. He wants me to play the part of the featherbrained Mrs. Feversham. I've never done anything like this. Frank says all I have to do is be myself. I don't know if he's being encouraging or sarcastic. Anyhow, I need your help."

"My help?"

"I need someone to read lines with me. Memorizing my part is easy. It's saying it aloud that petrifies me. It won't take much of your time. Please say you will," she begs.

I'm drowning in homework assignments. Calculus, advanced physics, geology, physiology, English. Impossible!

"Two weeks. That's all I ask. Fifteen minutes each day at The Ladies' Room. You're my only hope," she says, leaning close enough for me to see little beads of sweat forming on her upper lip.

I've never seen my older, wiser friend so desperate. Yet, there are all those assignments waiting for me. I'm tempted to tell her that I don't have the time. But that's what I said to Mary before her coming-out party.

"Of course, I'll do it," I say, frantically wondering where I'll find Jessie's fifteen minutes.

Her smile convinces me I've done the right thing. A second later she thrusts a copy of the script into my hands before crushing me with a giant hug.

The next day, she's waiting for me in a back corner of The Ladies' Room. We begin by going through the script together, page by page. She's already underlined her lines with red ink. We've only gone through a few pages when she glances at my face. "What's wrong?"

"Jessie, none of this makes any sense. It's ridiculous."

"As it should be."

"Then tell me in your own words. What's it about?"

"I'll try," she says, resting the copy of the script in her lap. "It's about love, and mistaken identity, silly disguises, and two newly married couples."

As Jessie explains the details, I cannot hold back. "Absurd!"

"Of course it's absurd. It's a farce. They're supposed to be silly."

While Jessie recites her lines, I play all the other parts. Now and then the girls in The Ladies' Room offer a sug-gestion. Her big moment, the fainting scene, has us all convulsed in laughter. We practice it several times. After the third go, Jessie finally remembers to place the back of her hand on her forehead before her collapse. Frank Norris made a brilliant casting choice. Everyone understands that by choosing this brilliant, serious woman to play the role of a silly lady, Frank has made his play even funnier. I'm laughing so hard I can hardly read my lines.

The laughter is good for me. There's a place for nonsense in the world. In fact, rather than feeling stressed from helping Jessie, I enjoy myself.

The play turns out to be everything one expects of a farce—a rip-roaring comedy of love and mistaken identity. We groan. We laugh. We shake our heads. It's a terrible play and yet hilarious. The audience howls in all the right places. Watching my smart, unflappable friend play the simpleton makes the play funnier.

Despite Jessie's witty performance, the thunderous applause, and the many floral bouquets tossed at her feet, in the end she vows to never do anything like this again. I, on the other hand, promise to allow a dose of silliness into my life.

With the farce over, the only time I ever see Jessie is in Professor Moses's lectures. But the arrival of a well-timed note from Ben Weed changes that.

December 10, 1892

Dear Julia,
To celebrate the end of exams, I'm organizing a hike into the hills. Frank Norris and Jessie Peixotto are coming. Be at Bacon Hall this Friday at noon.

*Pack a lunch. No need to reply. If I don't hear
from you, I'll assume you'll be there.*

*Your friend,
Benjamin Weed*

The morning of the hike, damp fog lingers over campus.
By noon, sunlight breaks through. The timing for this
tramp is good. Exams and papers are finished. Yes, I'm
more than ready for a change.

Chapter 25

THE HIKE

Arriving first, I check my rucksack. A cheese sandwich and apple are inside along with plenty of Smithy's famous snickerdoodle cookies, a sketchbook, and pencils. Minutes later Ben and Jessie arrive. Not surprisingly, Frank is late. He's consistently tardy for French class, never flustered or apologetic, always making a memorable entrance. When he finally arrives, he's wearing an overcoat long enough to skim the ground. Instead of a rucksack, he carries a briefcase along with a gold tipped walking stick.

"Hate hikes, old man," he says to Ben. "So, let's get this over with."

His rudeness shocks me, until I realize he's poking fun at Ben.

"Okay, troops. Let's move out," Ben barks, taking off in the direction of the hills above campus.

"Come on, Weed. Cut out that military talk," says Frank.

"You hate it, don't you?"

"Like poison."

The boys laugh. Jessie and I get the joke. Everyone knows that Frank has the reputation for being one of the worst cadets in the history of the college's military ranks. In fact, rumor has it that he's so bad at marching that his superior officers excuse him from the military parade.

"But you have a special flair, Frank," teases Jessie.

"I do my best," he says, standing at attention on a tree stump holding his walking stick like a flag, saluting smartly as we pass.

A few minutes later we are navigating a narrow winding path through shady eucalyptus groves.

"It's worth the effort," Ben assures us as we slog upward.

When we reach the clearing, winded and perspiring, we are rewarded with a breathtaking view. Below us we can see the entire bay including the tops of a few San Francisco buildings poking through a veil of fog.

Two downed eucalyptus logs offer the perfect picnic spot. Frank and I sit on one. Jessie and Ben choose the other, which is wrapped with bits of a dried-out red-leafed vine.

Digging through my rucksack, I bypass the sandwich in favor of my sketchbook. To my surprise, Frank pulls one from his briefcase. "Never travel without it," he says, waving his sketchbook in the air.

"Well, you two can draw all you like," Jessie says. "I'm hungry."

"Got an extra pencil in there, Julia?"

Inspecting the one I hand him, Frank takes a penknife from his pocket, and begins sharpening the point. He looks at me while he whittles.

"I've a proposal for you, Miss Morgan."

Familiar with Frank's love of mischief, I'm on guard.

"A contest. Ten minutes. That's it. Jessie and Ben will judge our work. Winner gets to keep the other's drawing."

I've seen his sketches in the campus newspaper. He's good, but so am I.

"I accept your terms, Mr. Norris. But I must warn you. Be prepared to hand over your drawing. It'll look quite nice on my wall."

"And yours will be smashing on mine."

He sets his pocket watch on the log.

"Ready? Go."

As I draw, the sounds of bird calls, squirrels scampering around tree trunks, and Ben and Jessie's voices fade. Before Frank proposed this drawing contest, I picked my subject. Across the bay is a gap between two points of land, where the bay empties into the vast ocean. At sunset, that gap is lit up by the last rays of the sun, a golden gateway. San Francisco sits on the left side. The focus of my drawing is on the right. My pencil dances across the paper.

"Time," Jessie shouts at exactly twelve fifty. "What've you got?"

We set our sketchbooks side by side against one of the logs. I'm surprised by the realism of Frank's sketch.

"Goat Island," he announces. "Over there." He points toward a small island near San Francisco. His shading captures the strange light perfectly.

Frank stands to explain his sketch. "I know the preferred name is Yerba Buena Island, but I'm terribly fond of goats. Please note the exquisite rendering of the four-legged creatures."

As they chat about Frank and his goats, I glance at my drawing.

Ravaging his sandwich in three bites, Frank says, "And yours, Julia?"

"Why Frank, do use your imagination."

Ben stands, and begins to pace in front of the drawings, hands behind his back, nose pointed upward. Clearing his throat, he begins a perfect imitation of Professor LeConte.

"Class, it is my opinion that in her drawing, Miss Morgan has captured an old Indian tale, one familiar to those of us who enjoy hiking these hallowed Berkeley hills."

"Why, Mr. Weed. How clever of you," I say. "You guessed my riddle."

"Yes, Miss Morgan. Your drawing of the Sleeping Maiden is exceedingly true. Now students, if you look over there, at the top of those hills on your right, you can see her." He points to the hills across the bay, in the direction of majestic Mount Tamalpais. "If you're clever, you can see the maiden's profile. She's on her back, sleeping of course. Her toes are there, those smaller hills to the left. Observe how her face, there on the right, looks skyward. Nice work, Miss Morgan."

After I'm declared the winner and tuck Frank's drawing into my rucksack, I pass Smithy's cookies around, rewarding Frank with an extra one for "good effort." As Jessie and Ben take theirs, I look closer at those vines on their log, the red leaves especially. While their scalloped edges resemble oak leaves, they are definitely not oak. These are growing in clusters of three. A single phrase leaps into my mind.

Repeating it aloud, I look at Ben. "*Leaves of three, leave them be.*"

Ben leaps up.

"What's wrong?" Jessie asks. "What did Julia say?"

"Up, Jessie. Stand up this minute," Ben shouts.

Puzzled, Jessie obeys. "Ben, are you trying to scare me?"

"No. It's just that we've made a terrible mistake." Looking my way, he says, "*Hairy vine, no friend of mine.*"

I nod. He gets it.

Ben is somber. "Poison oak, Jessie. This whole time you and I've been sitting on poison oak."

On a hike last fall, Sam accidently brushed his hand against some of those red leaves. Then he must have touched his face and scratched his tummy. Soon, the poor boy turned into a red, itchy nightmare. Needless to say, our lovely hike ended abruptly.

During the holiday break, Jessie sent me a letter divulging the gory details of her misadventure.

Of course, we washed our hands several times when we returned to campus. Unfortunately, that failed to keep me from breaking out with the most awful rash you can imagine. The doctor gave me a soothing ointment and wrapped my hands in cloths. I can only write to you now because the worst is over. I'm going to throttle that boy when I see him.

Chapter 26

UN-FAIR

In the drawing room, the only topic my fellow students want to talk about is the opening of the World's Columbian Exposition, otherwise known as The Chicago World's Fair.

How will they drain the swamp?

Will they be able to break through the frozen ground?

Will they finish in time?

Will the weather cooperate?

Architects and engineers from around the country are attempting miracles there. Today the talk is about the spectacular giant wheel designed by George Washington Gale Ferris, Jr.

I have studied the sketches of Ferris's wheel, which is higher than any existing building—more than 260 feet. It's breathtaking. The boys are skeptical.

Thirty-six cars, with forty people in each one. Impossible!

Picture windows for the view.

He's got four months to fit together over 100,000 pieces.

One mistake, and it'll crash down with thousands of people inside.

Even though he's using steel, it's much too flimsy.

And don't forget those Chicago winds.

Mr. Ferris's creation is designed to turn slowly, ending in a whisper stop. The boys are betting that Mr. Ferris will fail. I hope he succeeds, mainly to prove them wrong.

In a recent letter to Cousin Pierre, I raised the subject of the big wheel. While thrilling and creative, it strikes me as extraordinarily risky. Cousin Pierre disagrees. He believes Mr. Ferris's success will not only capture the world's attention but could lead to other engineering advances. "Think big, Julia," he admonishes.

I grin, ruminating on his gentle criticism. Thinking big is something I do every day, though my dreams do not include creating giant turning wheels.

Saph's buddy, Thomas Taylor, notices my smile.

"You look chipper today, Miss Morgan. Why don't you see if Mr. Ferris will hire you? I'm sure they need a perfectionist on their team."

His comment annoys me. I glance at his work. If anything, Taylor could use a dose of perfection. His pencil lines are askew, the lettering sloppy, and eraser dust litters his table.

On other days, when the boys are not going on about poor Mr. Ferris's wheel, they enjoy teasing me about the progress of the fair's Women's Building. Mostly they ridicule the idea of a building designed and then run entirely by women.

As usual, Taylor starts the razzing. "Miss Morgan. Are you planning to submit a design for the Women's Building?

I hear they can't find a decent woman architect. I suppose you're as qualified as any."

Taylor couldn't be more wrong. There are plenty of competent women architects. One, Louise Blanchard Bethune, rightly withdrew from the competition when she learned that she would be paid a tiny fraction of what the male architects would get for their plans.

I look up from my work. "If women were paid the same as men, my guess is that more women would submit plans."

"That'll never happen," he laughs. "Kind of like throwing good money after bad."

I'm silent, mainly because I don't know what to say. Later that week, when the boys begin their teasing about the Women's Building, I'm better prepared.

Steadying my T square to complete a line, I say, "Oh, I guess you haven't heard about Miss Sophia Hayden's winning design?"

"Who's she? An interior decorator?" Saph asks.

The boys laugh. I wait for them to quiet before going on. "Sophia Hayden happens to be a graduate in architecture from Boston College's Institute of Technology."

This shuts them up. The Institute enjoys a fierce reputation for rigor, and they know it.

Surprisingly, the Women's Building is the first completed at the fair, winning early praise. The critics applaud the interior for its delicacy of style, artistic taste, and elegance.

In my opinion, the outside of the building is equally magnificent, thanks to a San Francisco girl, Alice Rideout, who made news by adding sculptures of nude women. The boys in my class, bedazzled by the beauty of the figures, never utter a critical word about her graceful larger-than-life forms.

Still, the boys discover new ways to badger me.

"Not a bad looking building," one of the fellows says, "if you close your eyes."

"Poor thing," says another maliciously. "I heard Miss Hayden walked out at the end. Not up to it, I guess."

"Proves my point," Saph adds. "Women aren't cut out for that kind of work. Supervising construction is too strenuous for the fairer sex."

The real story weighs on me, the grim outcome replaying itself in my mind like a bad dream. I eat less and snap at everyone. Mary notices. At the end of lunch one day, she confronts me. "You've been crabby for days, Julia. What's going on? This isn't like you."

"I don't know how to explain it," I admit.

"Start from the beginning."

Mary follows me upstairs. When I open the door, Kat dashes into my room and onto my bed, her new favorite place. With Mary in the rocker by the window, and me next to Kat, it feels like old times. It turns out Mary knows something about the Chicago World's Fair, but not about the Women's Building.

"It's supposed to be designed by women, and it actually was, by Sophia Hayden. She's a brilliant architect, and barely older than us. Only twenty-one. Imagine that!"

"Impressive."

"She's achieved miracles in Chicago. Her building is beautiful."

"So, what's the problem?"

"She was fired."

"Fired? Why on earth . . . ?"

"Her boss, the chair of the Board of Lady Managers, is a woman used to getting her way."

"I smell trouble."

"You're right. That old bat invited her high-society friends to donate architectural features for the building."

"Sounds like a nice idea."

"Well, it wasn't. In no time the site was cluttered with hundreds of columns, window grills, sculptured figures, and doors. But here's the worst part. The chair demanded that Miss Hayden find a suitable place for every single one of those monstrosities."

"Oh, dear."

"It was terrible. When Miss Hayden complained, she was fired."

"How unfair."

"I agree," I say, heart racing. Kat purrs loudly from my brisk stroking.

"Couldn't she find a way to put all those things to good use?"

"Absolutely not. Look, Mary. It's like this. Let's say you write a story for the *Blue and Gold* newspaper, and one of those cocky editors tells you that it would be so much better if you added this or that, and soon, your story isn't your story anymore. Soon your story is a hodgepodge of ideas, and it's lost all its beauty, the main idea, the . . . "

"You've made your point, Julia. *Too many chefs spoil the pie.*"

"Broth, Mary! *Too many chefs spoil the broth.*"

But now a new thought nags at me. Someday, I could be in Miss Hayden's place. Would my clients treat me badly? I'm used to how the boys mistreat me, but coming from strangers it would be so much more hurtful. Until now, I never imagined those kinds of indignities. Now I wonder if being a woman makes me an easy target for constant insults. I never before doubted my decision to become an architect. Could I be making the biggest mistake of my life?

Chapter 27

THE GOAT

As I start my last year of college, I begin to wonder what I will do after graduation. I chase this thought away. In the meantime, I laugh at the senior boys and those few brave girls strutting around campus showing off their black plugs. I take pleasure in the news that Mr. Ferris's wheel is declared a stunning engineering achievement at the Chicago World's Fair.

I also welcome Emma to campus as a freshman and new member of Kappa Alpha Theta. Even though she looks healthy, cheeks plump, Mama and Papa insist that she live at home. This doesn't stop her from becoming a daily visitor to my room, mostly to chatter about Hart North.

"He wants to run for office, Dudu. Papa and I think he could win. I hate the idea of his being in Sacramento, though. Who'll escort me to all the dances and parties?"

I must also endure one last course with Professor Soulé. Despite his attitude about me, the class is fascinating. It's about predicting the strength of materials, like how long a beam should be or how high a brick wall can rise before weakening.

"You have until April to complete your senior thesis in this class," Professor Soulé announces. "It will focus on structural stress, determining centers of gravity, and the like. At the end of the year, you will all hand in a paper titled, 'Analysis of the Steel Framework of a Modern High Building.' I shall select one paper for special recognition. San Francisco's new Mills Building will be your subject. It's a steel frame skyscraper—an unheard-of ten stories high, the only one of its kind in the city. The architects are Burnham and Root."

Professor Soulé looks around the room. "Mr. Taylor. What can you tell us about Burnham and Root?"

"Head architects for the World's Fair, sir."

"And?"

Thomas turns beet red. Saph and I raise our hands. Saph gets the nod. "Skyscrapers, sir. They've built some of the tallest in the country, all in Chicago."

"Correct, Mr. Saph. Skyscrapers indeed. The Mills Building presents some fascinating opportunities for learning."

Soulé speaks over the swell of voices flooding the room. "Excuse me, class. I have not finished."

Silence.

"Now remember. This is a competitive thesis. Good luck to each of you."

Weeks later, Professor Soulé accompanies us on an inspection tour of the Mills Building. As he talks and jokes with the men during our ferry ride to San Francisco, I lean on the railing, recalling Cousin Pierre's words about his nearly finished eleven-story building. Mostly he complained about the huge number of workers he had to hire so he could stay on schedule.

I have an immense crew working for me. I also employ one person with a single job—to make sure there are enough workers on hand at all times. This is a complicated project, but efficiency saves me money. Wasting time on an enterprise like this cost a lot. My father's favorite saying these days is "Time is money."

I can imagine how the senior LeBrun keeps a close eye on his son's ambitious project. After all, this is LeBrun & Son's first skyscraper.

Work on the skyscraper requires considerable attention to such boring matters as cleaning up and restoring the neighborhood around our worksite. The immediate neighborhood is showing the wear and tear of our heavy-duty machinery. And the presence of thousands of workers only complicates the matter.

As we approach the Mills Building, I look for evidence of such wear and tear but see none. We gather at the front entrance while Professor Soulé points out exterior features, like the massive entry arch and the white marble that decorates the first two floors. The magnificence of the lobby silences the group. I run my hand along the cool black marble banister as I follow the curving staircase to the second floor where there are more marble columns and multicolored inlaid tiles.

While Professor Soulé accompanies a group to the basement, I join the group going to the roof. The elevator operator ushers us into a cagelike box. Slamming the bars shut, he stands with his back to us, his hand on the crank. I glimpse his smirk. He's used to the ride, knowing that we are not. The elevator takes off with a jolt, then shakes and rattles its way to the top, finally jerking to a stop. I'm so engrossed in studying the controls I don't realize how we are hanging hundreds of feet in the air. As we watch the elevator head back down to the first floor, I am eager to experience that return trip. From the green tint of the boys' faces, I guess they do not feel the same way.

Our hike up a staircase to the roof rewards us with an astonishing view of the city and bay, stark against the clear blue sky. I skirt the construction debris left behind including discarded scaffolding. A single plank extends several feet over the building's edge like a swimming pool diving board.

To my surprise, Taylor leaps atop the plank. Tilting his hat at a rakish angle, he grins at us then walks on the plank, arms outstretched, tightrope-walker style. Reaching the end, he turns around to salute us. I'm stunned. Taylor never struck me as a daredevil. Halfway back, he looks over the edge of the board. His smile vanishes.

"Come on back, Taylor," shouts Saph. "Don't clown around like that."

Taylor, now sheet-white and as rigid as the board under his feet, croaks, "Not clowning."

Saph yells again. "Cut it out, Taylor. You're scaring us."

Susan J. Austin + 169

"Don't mean to."

I lean over the edge of the building. What frightened Taylor? Ten floors down, the horse-and-carriages look like Sam's miniature toys. I've never been in a building so high. Fascinated, I lean farther over the edge for a better view, a small part of me delighting in Taylor's predicament.

Another shout. "Come on, Taylor. Stop fooling around."

Eyes wide, it is clear terror is paralyzing him. Surveying the boys, I wonder who will help their buddy? But no one steps forward. How pathetic. After several long agonizing minutes, it's clear that Taylor is not the only one frozen.

A frisky breeze tugs at my dress. Dust from the worksite swirls around my boots. Wind gusts playfully push against me, as if saying, "No time to waste." I feel the breeze strengthen. A few loose curls blow free from my bun.

As I near the plank, I congratulate myself for having the foresight to wear bloomers underneath my skirt. With a deep breath, I lift myself onto the plank as nimbly as if mounting my brothers' gymnastic equipment.

"Julia, are you crazy?"

No need to turn my head. I recognize Saph's whine.

"What are you doing? You can't go out there," another gasps.

I shut out their voices. Step by step, I inch my way to Taylor. His violent trembling vibrates the plank as he continues staring at the street below.

Softly, I say, "Taylor. Stop looking down. Walk toward me."

No reaction.

"Taylor, walk," I command

The board continues to shake.

"Look at me."

Nothing.

"Look at my eyes, my ears."

He continues to stare at the street below.

"Listen, Taylor. Put one foot in front of the other."

"C-c-c-can't."

"You can. Just do it. Look at me." I extend my hand.

"N-n-n-no!"

"Do it, Taylor."

"N-n-n-no!"

If he takes one step, I'm certain the next will be easier. One step. A sudden breeze puffs out my skirt. If it strengthens, we both run the risk of being blown off the plank.

I have one option. Scare him, but not too badly. Two words should do the trick.

"The Colonel."

"What?"

"The Colonel. He's on his way up," I lie.

Taylor moves his head the tiniest bit.

"You don't want Professor Soulé to see you like this, do you?"

Taylor lifts his head. His eyes meet mine. Slowly, very, very slowly, he reaches a trembling hand toward mine.

Professor Soulé never hears a whisper about Thomas's caper on the plank. I, on the other hand, earn a new nickname—*The Goat*, which I prefer to *digger*. When the men call me by my new name, I detect a hint of respect.

Chapter 28

A DOOR CRACKS OPEN

That semester, my fraternity gave me another new name—*Madame President*. This position always goes to a senior, and among the four of us, they selected me. They said I "get the job done." They said they liked the way I helped them choose our house colors, that I showed real leadership. They said I could be counted on. They said it was my sacred duty to accept this role. I understand *duty*. Mama made sure of that. Truth be told, I'm fond of these intelligent and spirited girls, and was pleased to become their president. However, there is little doubt I was a different sort, not as quick with a joke or funny story, not as eager to chitchat with everyone.

As president, I am awarded with the largest of the seven bedrooms. The massive table in the corner proved to be excellent for drawing as well as for stacking piles of fraternity paperwork. Bright light pours in from the corner-room windows.

"Of course, you were the best choice," Mary assured me on one of her visits to my new bedroom. "You're the most organized person I know. And when you talk, even if it's not very loud or very often, we listen."

"Is that supposed to encourage me?"

Mary bounced a few times on the edge of my bed, disturbing Kat's nap. "Pretty nice, Madame President."

As our Theta calendar fills, I keep records for each event, and there are several. There are guest lists to make, invitations to send, balance sheets to show what we spend and what money we take in. We buy supplies and we hire bands for our dances as well as extra help to cook, serve guests, and clean.

College has prepared me for this. I can accurately estimate the amount of time for each task, how much I can fit into any given day or week, and how much more I can take on. I also figure out how to cut our meeting times in half.

Everyone knows what to do, and by when. We work together like a well-oiled machine. What surprises me most is how much I enjoy it, even those teas and cozies. Perhaps I tolerate them better because now I have a special role to play instead of making idle chitchat.

I can tell the girls approve of me. The younger ones are the first to volunteer. The older ones rarely argue or complain about their assignments.

I also notice a slight but significant change in my fellow engineering students. They are far less surly, offering occasional smiles or friendly greetings. And I don't mind when they use my new nickname, *The Goat*. Any kind of greeting is better than none at all. And then, several months into the semester, a door cracks open that I'm keen to walk through.

These days my time is consumed with the Mills project. There are endless calculations and building diagrams to complete, all work I enjoy. As usual, I'm absorbed by the smallest detail. Most afternoons I race up to the drawing room where I share a workspace with Arthur Brown, my old high school classmate. He, too, is majoring in engineering, though a year behind me.

One day Professor Soulé pays a surprise visit along with a stranger. The professor, assuming his familiar military posture, back straight, hands clasped behind his back, calls for our attention. All chatter ceases.

"I have a special guest today, an architect. Thought I'd show him around. Pay us no mind. Carry on," he commands with a flick of his wrist.

I watch the visitor circle the room as he studies our drawings pinned to the walls. A full beard frames his round face. A black beret is perched on his head, set at a rakish angle. His bright eyes and genuine smile remind me of a large, friendly bear. After the two men circle the room, they walk down the aisles, their eyes never straying from our work. The quiet is unsettling. The only sounds are pencils scratching on paper. Eventually, Professor Soulé stops at Saph's table.

The architect moves ahead, stopping by Arthur and me. He studies Arthur's work.

"May I?"

"Yes, sir," Arthur nods.

The man puts his finger on the corner of the diagram Arthur has labored over for the past hour, eraser dust scattered everywhere. "If you shave off this edge by an eighth of an inch, I think you'll like what you see."

"I'll do that, sir," Arthur replies. "Thank you."

The man then turns his attention to my work. "Nice. Steel is it?"

"Yes, sir."

I'm about to describe our Mills Building assignment when Professor Soulé joins him. Arthur and I stand.

"Mr. Arthur Brown and Miss Julia Morgan. Let me introduce you to Mr. Bernard Maybeck."

He turns to Mr. Maybeck. "Young Mr. Brown here is interested in architecture. Apparently, this is also true for Miss Morgan, but I'm guessing it's more likely a passing fancy before she settles down." Addressing both of us, he says, "Mr. Maybeck and I have been talking about starting an architectural program here. Ah, but I'm afraid that will be after you graduate, Miss Morgan."

So like Professor Soulé. That's how he feels about all the women here—a passing fancy. But did he say there may be an architect on faculty . . . here . . . next fall? And I'm missing it? What terrible luck.

To Arthur, he says, "Mr. Maybeck works for the architectural firm of Arthur Page Brown. May I presume that Mr. Brown is no relation of yours?"

Arthur grins. "You're right, he's not, but there's a third Arthur Brown. My father—Arthur Brown Senior, a builder of railway bridges and ferries among other things. As a matter of fact, he was the architect for the Hotel Del Monte in Monterey. Maybe you've heard of it."

I look at Arthur with new interest. I'm familiar with his father's work but am astonished to hear he designed the elegant Del Monte, one of the finest hotels anywhere. My family will be vacationing there this summer.

Several weeks later, I notice an envelope pinned onto the Civil Engineering bulletin board, addressed in elegant script to *Miss Julia Morgan*. There is a second envelope for *Mr. Arthur Brown*.

Arthur arrives as I'm slitting mine open.

"Invite to a party?" he asks.

"I don't think so."

We read our cards in silence.

"Well, I'll be," Arthur says, eyes wide. "Are you going?"

"Of course," I reply, more cheerful than I've felt for ages.

It's an invitation to a series of discussions on architectural design, hosted by Mr. Bernard Maybeck at his home in Berkeley. The seminar will not officially begin until the fall, but in the meantime, would we please come to his home next week to learn more?

I'm surprised Mr. Maybeck included me after Professor Soulé's humiliating introduction. It would be perfectly reasonable for him to think I was one of those girls who attended college to meet a husband. Why should he waste his time on me?

For the last few years, I have been dreaming of creating a building based entirely on my own ideas. We rarely discuss design in my engineering classes. This seminar couldn't be better timed. Of course, there is the matter of my parent's approval, but I brush that thought aside. I will be content to attend Mr. Maybeck's gathering next week.

Seven of us squeeze into his tiny one-story cottage north of campus. Mr. Maybeck begins with a surprising announcement. "My modest home is soon to undergo a transformation. Next fall, with your help, I will have a set of expansion plans for my little abode."

I pay close attention. He's dressed differently from when he visited campus. Now, a Chinese-style jacket hangs over baggy pants. I catch glimpses of Mrs. Maybeck, also dressed in a curious fashion. Her dress is made from a combination of fabrics—lacy sleeves, bits of satin and velvet sewn on in surprising places. I have little doubt Mama would not approve.

"This seminar will be practical," Mr. Maybeck explains. "We're going to learn about architecture by actually building those additions to my cottage. You'll experience something you can never learn from a book." Eyes twinkling, he adds, "And of course, with your help, Mrs. Maybeck and I will have a substantially larger dwelling."

As he explains the particulars of his seminar, I'm so enthralled I cannot write straight. Soon, I stop taking notes altogether, listening instead to his every word. We move outside to sketch neighboring houses. As we draw, Maybeck points out features I've never thought about, like setting, the slope of the ground, and style.

This brilliant and passionate teacher is electrifying. Drawing at a furious pace, I enter a brand-new world.

Unlike Arthur, who asks question after question, I am silent, but Mr. Maybeck's words haunt me: "Think about houses simply built that use shadows as ornaments instead of those wood ornaments so over-used these days. And one more thing. If wood is used, it should look like wood, not stone."

I think back on my old high school and how its wood decorations went up in flame. Mr. Maybeck is suggesting something different.

He talks about roof angles and the placement of windows, starting several sentences with, "As I learned at the École des Beaux-Arts . . . " This isn't the first time I have heard mention of this school. Cousin Pierre's most-recent letter also refers to the École.

That evening I reread it. For the longest time, I stare at the part he underlined.

January 24, 1894

Dear Julia,
Your list of courses is indeed exciting. We have discussed how your degree in engineering will prepare you well for your next steps. My architecture colleagues speak highly of a school in Paris, the École des Beaux-Arts. I'd look into it, if I were you.

Tucking the letter away, I take out my best writing paper. With graduation a few months away, I need a plan. For a start, I will inquire about enrolling in the drawing classes at San Francisco's new Art Institute.

After sealing my letter to the Institute, I begin a second that explains my summer plans to Mama and Papa. A few days later two letters arrive in the post. One is from the Institute welcoming me to their classes. The other is from Mama. "A sensible idea," she writes. "Drawing classes should make for an enjoyable summer."

I did not mention the Maybeck seminar. No need to hurry things. Sometimes, the less my parents know the better.

Chapter 29

A JOLLY GOOD CROWD

The last Theta tea of the year will be to honor Mrs. Hearst. It promises to be our biggest and most ambitious. Thanks to the flower committee, every surface of the house displays a colorful bouquet. Mama loaned us Grandmother's silver teapot with its tray, sugar, and creamer, all polished mirror bright.

The girls line the path, welcoming Mrs. Hearst to Theta House. She's elegantly attired, wearing a flowered hat that suits the occasion. As president, I stand at the top of the stairs.

"Miss Morgan," she says warmly.

"Mrs. Hearst. Welcome to Kappa Alpha Theta."

She compliments the beauty of our house, sits in our best chair, and samples dainty tea sandwiches. I catch Smithy peering at the great lady from the kitchen doorway. Our housemother, Mrs. Lee, wears her "good dress," a simple but elegant black frock saved for special occasions.

I manage to eat a sandwich and the last chocolate-covered cherry. In the midst of all this hubbub, Kat enters, tail held high.

Frantically, Mary tugs my arm. "Julia. Kat."

I'm surprised. Our tiny tiger usually steers clear of gatherings.

"Good for Kat."

"No, Julia. Not good. She's brought a present."

"A present?"

"Look."

Prancing toward Mrs. Hearst, Kat dangles a stunned tiny brown mouse from her mouth. Mary and I exchange horrified looks. Will Kat drop her furry victim at the feet of our guest of honor? Probably. She's done it before. Mary positions herself between me and Mrs. Hearst, trying to block Mrs. Hearst's view of Kat. I sweep the little troublemaker into my arms, the mouse still locked in her jaws. Silently, I hand Kat off to Smithy, who disappears into the kitchen, the door swinging behind her. I sneak a glance at Mrs. Hearst, holding her gloved hand in front of her mouth, suppressing a laugh. She must be familiar with the whims of cats.

By the time Mrs. Hearst departs, she has exchanged a few private words with each senior girl.

Afterward, Mary and I collapse on the couch, watching our freshmen sisters move the furniture back into place, Emma working as hard as the others.

The softness of the couch cradles my weary body. It's not the planning for these events that exhausts me. It's making conversation. A few minutes on the couch should perk me up. A long night of study awaits. Despite working nonstop on my thesis, the clock is ticking.

Mary unbuttons her boots. "Ah, that feels good. Of course, undoing this corset would feel even better."

"How true. As soon as you leave, that's exactly what I intend to do."

"You can't get rid of me that easily, Julia Morgan. What did you and Mrs. Hearst talk about?"

"Oh, this and that."

"Come on, Julia."

"No. You first."

"Well, she remembered that I wanted to teach," Mary says, smoothing her skirt. "She suggested I think about teaching in one of the women's colleges."

"A sound idea."

"I agree. I even have a few in mind." Mary looks at me. "Okay, your turn."

"We had a lovely conversation about Paris."

This word has a magical effect. Mary studies my face as if it holds answers to a mystery.

"Paris?"

"Yes, Paris. Mrs. Hearst thinks highly of the École des Beaux-Arts."

I've told Mary about the few architectural schools in America, but I've never mentioned the École. The idea seems so far-fetched. Despite my fatigue, I welcome this conversation, one I've had only in letters to Cousin Pierre and in my head.

"Julia, are you really thinking of studying in Paris?"

"Perhaps. Mrs. Hearst isn't the only one to suggest it."

"Who else?"

"Mr. Maybeck. He studied there. According to him, there's no better place in the world. Pierre LeBrun is also keen on it. There is one small problem though." I pause to absorb the enormity of my next words. "In their long history, they've never admitted a woman."

Mary sits up. "Wait! You're thinking about going to a school that doesn't allow women? My word, Julia. You do love a challenge, don't you?"

While Mary lists all the reasons why I should give the École a try, I wonder how I could be thinking of enrolling in yet another school where I am unwelcome.

"I'd listen to them, Julia. If anyone can do this, it's you." She smiles then nudges me with her elbow. "Do you believe us?"

"What?"

"Jabbering on about life after college. Feels like yesterday when we had that last skate." She squeezes my hand. "Now look at us. All grown up."

"Slow down, Mary. We have one more youthful extravagance ahead. And I don't know how to wiggle out of it."

"The Pageant?"

I nod. "Frank and Jessie cornered me last week. Their script includes musical interludes. They want me to play my violin with a few others."

"And you should. They've been working hard. I'm helping with costumes. The class of '94 will make history with this one. You'll see."

"First things first. There's my thesis to finish. And something called final exams."

"You'll be fine, Julia. You always are."

And I knew she was right. I had hesitated attending Mary's coming-out party and by doing so, nearly ended our friendship. And why? Because of my worries about doing a less-than-perfect job with my schoolwork. I helped Jessie with the Junior Farce when she needed me, and though it meant working even harder in some classes, it was worth seeing her smile. I devoted hours as Theta president, in large part because I genuinely like these girls. The Senior Pageant offers yet another opportunity for me to place friendship before work. I promise myself to do whatever I can for the Class of 1894.

As Mary launches into the details of the pageant, my eyes droop. Her voice fades. Sometime later, when I awake, Mary is gone. Kat is curled at my side. Hushed conversation drifts from the dining room where light supper is being served. I stretch my arms, swallow and freeze. No! It can't be. A sore throat? Not now. Predictably, all my scratchy throats turn into colds. I push the idea away. I cannot get sick now.

After a fitful night I awake to another familiar sensation—a hammer-like pounding in my ear. The dull, throbbing pain goes on and on. I hear Mama's voice echo in my head. "Rest, Dudu." But I cannot. So much to do. Exams. My thesis. I must push through.

No one knows my agony. No one knows how the pain keeps me awake night after night. While I'm quieter than usual, spending more hours in my room, my fraternity sisters leave me alone.

The exams are no problem. I've kept up on my classwork, but my thesis requires several diagrams as well as challenging mathematical computations. On the last possible day, when I finally hand my paper to Professor Soulé, he places it on the pile already stacked on his desk.

"Miss Morgan. This is a surprise. It's not like you to be so close to a deadline." He thumps the pile with his knuckles. "Too difficult?"

"No, sir."

"Not your cup of tea, I suppose. Which reminds me. I understand Mr. Maybeck has invited you to his seminar. Suits you better than studying reinforced concrete in sky-scrapers. By the way, he's definitely joining the faculty in the fall."

I long to discuss the advantages of combining steel and concrete with Professor Soulé, and I'm delighted that Mr. Maybeck will be teaching here. But my throbbing ear does not permit this conversation.

"That's nice," is all I manage to say, defeated by pain.

A week later I see Saph lounging on the North Hall steps, his buddies slapping him on the back, shaking his hand. There are shouts of congratulations. I suspect he has won the competition for best thesis. I'm further convinced when he fails to tease me as I walk by.

I know my paper is top-notch, but I also did not expect to win. Over the last four years, I've grown accustomed to getting grades lower than the other engineering students. Even so, I'm at the top of my class. The few times I glimpsed Saph's drawings, I had two impressions. One, he draws well. Two, he avoids risk by keeping things simple.

During those last few days of back-to-back exams, my ear continues its torture. Sleep is fitful. The pain finally ebbs on the last day of exams. Exhausted, I spend the weekend at home, sleeping. Monday morning, I'm back at school. Senior Week preparations have begun.

"Fitz wrote all the music for the pageant," Jessie assures

me as she describes the script. "All you have to do is play with the others."

If Fitz McCoy wrote the music, it will be first rate. A violinist, he's the creative genius behind most of the musical productions for my class. But can I rise to his standards? I memorize my part in a few days, and soon Thetas are humming Fitz's melodies.

As the class of '94 gathers on the steps of the Mechanical Arts Building for our one rehearsal, we are aware of the uniqueness of our senior pageant. Ben Weed is partly responsible. Every year the pageant takes place on campus in front of one of the buildings. It's crowded and impossible for the audience to see or even hear what's going on.

Ben's discovery changes all this. Jessie fills me in on the details. "It's perfect, Julia. Frank and I were there last week. It's not far away, has a perfect slope, and is big enough for our pageant plus the audience. You'll see."

"But did he check for poison oak?"

"I hope so, or else there'll be lots of people who will never talk to him again."

As I join the ninety-five members of my class zigzagging our way up a narrow path to the site, I watch for exposed tree roots and gopher holes, my violin tucked safely under my arm. The path ends in a secluded eucalyptus grove with a large clearing. Thick shade, combined with the familiar spicy fragrance, adds to enclosure's magic. Ben's discovery is indeed brilliant. The ground slope offers the audience a clear view. Plucking a few strings of my violin, I appreciate how the setting beautifully amplifies sound.

Frank Norris, our writer and director, calls Ben to the front. "To honor finding this superb place, we hereby bestow upon it the following name—The Ben Weed Amphitheater."

Shouts of "huzzah!" and "well done!" echo throughout the grove. Frank's enthusiasm infects us all.

"The altar will be here," he says, climbing atop the huge round stump of a downed eucalyptus tree. "Now, divide into two groups on either side of it—east side there and west side over there." Pointing east he adds, "Musicians there. Remember, there'll be a fire on the altar, so stay downwind of the smoke."

The rehearsal is hilarious. The tension and stress of the last several weeks evaporate like a morning fog.

One job remains—for the women to create ninety-five brown-hooded monk robes. For the next several days we crowd into the Ladies' Room along with bolts of brown fabric, cutting tables, and two sewing machines Jimmie Tait tracked down.

My job is to draw the patterns. We finish the last robe two days ahead of schedule. My newly acquired class spirit amuses me. When we all recite the final chant at the conclusion of the pageant, I'm as rowdy as the others. The eucalyptus grove vibrates with our raucous shouts:

Of the Class of '94, my friends, the Class of '94,
There never'll be one as great again, there never
was one before;
And all shall know where'ere we go, as all have
known as yore,
Oh, we're a jolly good crowd, for we're the Class
of '94.

Mama, Papa, Emma, Avery, and Sam attend the graduation ceremonies in Harmon Gymnasium. Only Parmelee is absent. He's traveling, trying to decide what to do with his life. We all hope he finds an answer.

While the graduation speeches drone on, I study the program where Augustus Valentine Saph is listed as winner for the most outstanding thesis. I look for the positive side. *Am I not the only woman to graduate in engineering this year and at the top of my class? Saph can have his award. Other challenges surely await me, but for now I'll enjoy the moment.*

Three days later I'm back in my Oakland bedroom, once again under Mama's roof, but I'm not the only graduate. Avery finished high school.

My summer is planned. Between art classes and a week with my family at the Del Monte Hotel in Monterey, I will be busy. Mr. Maybeck's seminar starts afterward, and my parents have yet to give their approval. I remind myself how Jessie waited years for her father's permission to attend college. *Patience, Julia*, I tell myself.

But every time I bring up the seminar, it's the same thing. "We'll see."

When I push Mama further, she launches into a speech I've heard a million times. "Dudu, you must understand how the seminar interferes with the most important time of your life. I'd hate to see you completely ruin your chances for marriage and lifelong happiness. You don't want to jeopardize everything, do you?"

"But Mama, this is a rare opportunity for me to learn about architectural design from an extraordinary teacher."

"No doubt, but you're not getting any younger, are you?"

Mama is right, of course. I'm not getting younger. Being twenty-two and unmarried is not an enviable position. By now, most of my high school girlfriends who chose marriage over college are having their first babies. And the daily post includes wedding announcements from my college chums.

My parents have always supported me. For how long can I count on that?

Chapter 30

PILE OF BRICKS

On a free day in June, I invite Avery to walk with me to the new high school. As we head downtown, thick summer fog blocks out the tiniest sliver of sunlight.

"I enjoyed your violin performance at the pageant. First rate," Avery offers.

"That's kind of you, Avery, but I'm amazed you could pick me out in that mob." I wrap my shawl tighter against the chilly air.

"It was easy. I just looked for the shortest brown-robed monk with a violin."

Avery, tall and lanky, glances at me. A grin replaces his usual solemn look. Not long ago, he was an irritable two-year-old who never stopped crying. Now that cranky rascal is a tall, handsome young man.

As we near Oakland's new high school, I remember holding Sam's hand as we watched fire gobble up the top floor of that ornate wooden monstrosity called our school. The second fire left more damage. Patched up, it limped along for almost four years—until now.

"Goodness, Avery, they've built a fortress!"

"But decent looking," he says.

A mammoth four-story solid brick building fills the entire square block.

"It's already got a nickname," Avery says as he leads me up one of two exterior staircases to the first floor. "Old Pile of Bricks."

I'm not surprised. Eventually, everything earns a nickname around here—people, and even buildings.

"First on our tour is one of my favorite places," Avery says as we climb a broad interior central staircase to the top floor, floor-to-ceiling windows lighting our way. With students and teachers away for the summer, the halls are eerily quiet.

He leads the way through a wide hallway ending with double doors. Throwing open one, he shouts, "Ta-da!"

"A gymnasium!" I exclaim.

An unheard-of luxury when they built our old building. I catch the lingering smell of fresh varnish from the highly polished floor.

"Nice, Avery. But you know what I really want to see."

"Coming right up."

Down the hall we enter Miss Connors's mechanical arts drawing room, more spacious than the old one, but absent my teacher.

A week later I return, hoping to run into Miss Connors. This time I'm in luck. She's in her classroom, sorting through piles of student projects.

"Miss Morgan, what a pleasant surprise," she says, smiling.

I recall my first impression of this formidable woman

eight years ago, when I was a new high school pupil. Except for a few gray hairs, she looks the same.

After polite small talk, I bring up Mr. Maybeck's invitation, then move to the heart of the matter. "While I graduated in engineering, it's architecture I really care about."

"Of course, it is."

"Attending Mr. Maybeck's seminar is what I've been hoping for. My parents are on the fence."

Miss Connors holds a drawing up to the light then turns it around for me to see. It is a crude, clumsy attempt. We shake our heads.

"I've struggled with this student all year," she says, placing it face down. "I'm sure your parents will come around, Miss Morgan."

But you don't know them. Taking this seminar is more complicated than it sounds. Mama's worried. Her eldest daughter, still unwed? The shame.

"I hope you're right. I've been trying to sort out what to do next. My future."

Those two words hang in the air. *My future.*

"I've been encouraged to study architecture at the École de Beaux-Arts in Paris."

"The École is an outstanding school, Miss Morgan. But isn't it *men only*?"

"It is. But that might change."

"Indeed?"

Miss Connors stops sorting papers, her hands now still. I speak longer and faster than intended. " . . . It's true. The École has never admitted a woman. . . . And, of course, I can't help wondering, why me? . . . It could be a waste of my time. . . . I'd only get there to be turned away. . . . And there's the expense. . . . And even if I got in, what makes me think I can succeed?"

Miss Connors says nothing.

"There's a rumor, ma'am. Women artists are insisting on admission to the École's art school. Of course, that's not the architecture school but . . . "

She leans forward. "You're right. Paris does indeed sound like a gamble."

Her words pierce me like arrows. Until then, I was unaware of how desperately I wanted to go.

"But Miss Morgan, consider this. If those women artists succeed in getting accepted, you shall benefit."

She's right, of course, but am I willing to take the risk? The boys' nickname for me is well chosen. Like the goat, I like knowing where to place my hooves before taking a step.

"Miss Morgan. There's something else. To triumph at the École requires extraordinary qualities. You have those."

Miss Connors must be exaggerating. How unlike her.

"Three come to mind. First, of course, is ability. You draw exceedingly well. You proved your skills in high school, and of course at college. Top of the class. My, my."

Ability. Yes, she's right. I know I can do the work.

"Then there's persistence. You redid your work more times than most, and you didn't stop until it was right. And, of course, the boys did their best to rattle you. I'm happy to say, with little success."

She knew all along what I had endured.

"Don't look so shocked, Miss Morgan. I'm not blind. I saw their misdeeds. All those supposed accidents. Those slights." She shifts her weight in the chair. "I saw them because I was treated the same way when I was a student."

What a relief to know that there are other women like me, dealing with rude, unkind men.

Miss Connors fiddles with her stack of papers before going on. "And finally, Miss Morgan, there's ambition. It's not a word we feel comfortable using for women. I know that. We're not supposed to be ambitious. We're told it's unbecoming. The fact is, without ambition, you can't survive. But you have ambition. I've seen it. You don't let anything keep you down."

Is it ambition that explains the hunger that drives me to work hard, to succeed against such tremendous odds? Miss Connors is right. Ambition is a word reserved for men. Of course, Mama has her own opinion on the subject. To her, the only way a girl can achieve true happiness is to have ambition knocked out of her.

Chapter 31

THE PATH

Arm in arm, Mary and I take one last stroll past our giant Monterey pine, the place where we had our most important talks. Tomorrow, she leaves for New York on the train with her parents. We will not see each other again for ages.

As usual, I find myself saying things to Mary that I would normally keep to myself. "Dear me, Mary. If I can't get my parents to agree on Mr. Maybeck's seminar, how in the world will they ever say yes to France?"

"*A step at a time*, my friend. *A step at a time.*"

I hear the voice of the teacher she dreams of becoming. She's already sent letters of inquiry to colleges seeking teachers. And then there's a certain young man who makes Mary's eyes sparkle, the older brother of one of our fraternity sisters.

"Remember to take your own wise advice, my friend. *A step at a time.* Warren will wait for you if you two are meant to be together."

"You're right. We both have things to do."

Her smile gives her away. She is more than fond of him.

"He'll be waiting for you, I'm sure."

"It's rather funny, isn't it Julia? Me, traveling on the Transcontinental Railway. And don't fret, I'll wave at your bridge when I arrive."

"Of course you will, but don't just look at it. Walk across the beast. I guarantee you the thrill of a lifetime."

As the days go by, I look for a sign that my parents have come to a decision. In the midst of their wavering, the worst happens. Mama and Papa visit friends who recently moved to Berkeley. Mama's report is alarming. "The house is lovely, Dudu, and so spacious. We had tea on their veranda, behind their wisteria vine. It's blooming. Purple flowers everywhere. What a fragrance! A most pleasant visit. And guess who walked by?"

"Who?"

"Mr. and Mrs. Maybeck."

"Are you sure?"

They've never met the Maybecks. How would they know?

"Oh, it was them alright. Quite the conspicuous couple, I must say. Even rather extraordinary."

As Mama describes the moment, her fan speaks louder than her words, fluttering hummingbird fast.

"It seems everyone in Berkeley knows them. Such an odd couple, and what mystifying attire. Why would anyone dress in such an outrageous fashion? Mr. Maybeck's jacket had one of those Chinese collars. His hat was the kind you'd see in Scotland. Plaid, flat, and with a pom-pom on top. And Mrs. Maybeck. Such a gaudy dress, patched together like a quilt."

Fingering the locket Mary gave me as a farewell gift, I'm determined to make light of the situation. "Oh, Mama, they're artists and practical people. That's all."

Still, the timing couldn't be worse. Mama cares about how people present themselves. This could ruin everything.

As our summer vacation nears, I'm resigned to leave without a clear picture of my future. Lately, I have the pleasant daydream of imagining a life that doesn't require my parents' approval for everything. But I'm also a realist. I do depend on their financial help.

Sam and Avery are off camping with friends, and Parm is in the east, so it's just four of us going—Papa, Mama, Emma, and me.

Of course, Emma is sad to leave her beau, Hart North. She chose well. He's bright and ambitious. Finishing law school as promised, his campaign for a seat in the California assembly is heating up. He may actually win.

Our trip to Monterey is long and tiring. We endure assorted transfers—carriage rides, a ferry crossing, and my favorite, a three-and-a-half-hour train trip on the Del Monte Express beginning with magnificent views of the white-capped Bay. One of the few stops is San Jose. As our train inches through the bustling downtown area, warning gongs clang at every corner. Horse-drawn carriages clog the streets.

Emma is first to spot the city's astonishing landmark—a 250-foot metal tower straddling Market Street. The bottom is wide enough for several carriages to travel through, side by side. The top supports a powerful electric arc that at night can be seen for miles.

"Don't you think it looks a lot like Mr. Eiffel's tower in Paris?"

"Oh, Dudu, you always say that." Emma laughs.

"I suppose you're right, but I can't help wondering . . . "

"I know. You think Mr. Eiffel visited San Jose ages ago, saw the tower, and then went back to Paris to design his own."

"I do. After all, his went up eight years later. It's perfectly logical."

Grabbing my sketchbook, I draw the tower. Cousin Pierre must see this. He's certain to agree with my conclusion about this bizarre coincidence.

Soupy fog follows us all the way to the Del Monte depot. As I climb down the train steps, I take a deep breath. The air is lightly perfumed by the sea. A brightly painted wagon awaits us, enclosed and able to carry a dozen hotel guests. Two stately horses with braided manes and tails stand at the front, raising and lowering their hooves, impatient to leave. We climb inside through doors at the rear and sit on benches running along its sides.

The ride to the hotel is both eerie and beautiful. Damp, seaborne fog dances in and out, hiding lichen-covered Monterey pines and gnarled cypress trees perched on seaside cliffs. The final curve takes us under a natural canopy created by twisted cypress branches. As we pull in front of the enormous three-story hotel, brilliant sunshine chases away the last traces of fog. Men and women in elegant hats and summer whites lounge on the glass-enclosed sunporch that wraps around the front and sides of the main building.

Emma and I share a third-floor room at the front of the hotel. From here I can survey the hotel's famous green hedge maze, its confounding paths hidden from view. Most of the next day I draw seascapes and write letters.

Before I start Cousin Pierre's, I reread his most recent.

June 7, 1894

Dear Julia,
Congratulations on your graduation! From that day we stood on the Brooklyn Bridge, I knew you showed promise. You were only eleven, but I was right.

As usual, I'm thinking about your future. You know what I'm going to say, because I've said it before. Please consider attending the École. Each time I mention this, you write back all the reasons why it won't work. Nevertheless, I think you should try.

In my letter I thank him for his confidence, promise to consider the École, and then describe the San Jose tower including my suspicions about Mr. Eiffel. Folding my drawing into quarters, I slip it in the envelope with my letter.

Next, I write to Miss Connors. How fortunate to have such a good friend—tough, clear-eyed, and supportive.

Sealing both letters, I'm distracted by shouts and laughter. A high-spirited crowd gathers around the giant maze's exit. Probably another "rover" has gone astray. All day I hear shouts from lost guests wandering the twisting mile-long pathway, unable to find their way out.

"We're coming. We're coming. Hold your horses,"

shouts a groundsman, lugging an eight-foot ladder stashed nearby for such occasions.

I take a moment to consider the maze. The walls, constructed of impenetrable Monterey cypress, are about seven feet high and as wide as I am tall—just under five feet. Planted close together, the trees form a thick, solid hedge. The garden crew clips them into pristine shape every day.

How could someone get so lost that they feel compelled to accept help from a man shouting directions from a tall ladder? Watching hotel guests laugh and yell encouragement to their lost comrade provokes my interest. That could never happen to me. Or could it?

I decide to find out but do my "homework" first. After walking around the exterior of the maze, I arrive at several conclusions:

The creator of the maze has a keen sense of humor. Five-foot-high castles, knights, rooks, and pawns crafted from the sculptured cypress hedge bestow a comic touch. A giant chess game. I'm good at chess.

I shall not leave behind a trail of colored thread or paper scraps to mark where I've been, like those other rovers. Hansel and Gretel left a trail of cookie crumbs and look what happened to them.

My height puts me at a disadvantage. The hedge walls tower above my head, so I shall not be able to use the sculptured archways framing both the entrance and exit as a clue.

No matter how long it takes to find my way to the exit, I will *not* shout for assistance.

When I step into the maze the next morning, I'm surrounded by the hedges' cooling shade. I note the exact location of the sun, knowing that it travels from east to west. Tracking the sun's movement will be helpful.

I could keep my hand on the right hedge wall from beginning-to-end as a kind of guide, but that is a mindless method, much like using those paper scraps and colored threads. Instead, I utilize that unique skill I realized on my first day in Miss Connors's class. As I walk through the maze, I create a complete map in my mind's eye of where I've been.

An hour later, after an occasional dead end and bothersome backtracking, I arrive at the exit. Smiling, I think about those poor bewildered men and women I left behind. A few made a desperate attempt to scramble over the hedges, only to fail miserably.

Emma and I made plans to meet on the front steps of the hotel once I complete the maze. Our plan? A tramp through the cypress groves and along the ocean-side cliffs. I promised to be there at noon, exactly. Her job was to secure a picnic lunch from the kitchen.

She is there, picnic basket in hand. "Well, Dudu. You look like the cat that ate the canary. I take it you won the battle of the maze?"

"Indeed. A nice warm-up for our walk. Most invigorating."

We follow a path through a nearby cypress grove.

"Oh, there's one, Dudu. Just right for you."

A gnarled stick the length of a cane lay on the ground, discarded by a hiker. The knob on the top feels good in my hand. A few steps farther we spot a longer one for Emma.

Exiting the grove an hour later, the pungent smell of the sea fills my nostrils. A gentle breeze sways a field of golden poppies, bright against the blue-green ocean below.

I point ahead. "Over there. That's our place."

A lone cypress tree at the cliff's edge offers filtered shade and an expansive view of the white surf and jagged rocks below. Best of all, we are alone, not a person in sight. I'm suddenly famished. Our lunch of cold chicken, cheese, and bread, ending with one of the hotel's famous peach turnovers, is quickly eaten. I stretch out on my back, place my straw hat over my eyes, and within seconds fall into a deep sleep.

A sudden chill wakens me. Opening my eyes, I'm overwhelmed by a peculiar feeling. Someday I will live in this enchanted place of peace and tranquility. This bay with its gnarled trees, high cliffs, and forever changing colors will be my refuge. How and when is a mystery, but I am as certain as Papa enjoying two desserts at dinner, Mama scolding him, and Emma laughing into her napkin.

On our walk back, Emma heads toward the hotel. I make my way to the splendid, crescent-shaped Lake El Estero. Hotel guests are rowing boats or strolling nearby. Ahead, I see a bridge of stone and wood stretching across the lake, high enough for boats to pass under.

Heading toward the bridge, I recall how Mary and I spent hours floating leaves in small streams. I select a likely candidate but what shall be its passenger? Reaching into a pocket, my fingers touch a smooth acorn tucked away months ago. As soon as I set the little acorn on the leaf and into the water, they are swiftly carried away. Rushing ahead to the bridge, I lean over its edge and watch the leaf with its precious cargo sail towards me.

The acorn's ride is rough and perilous as it bumps into small rocks and twigs along the way, but it never stops or veers off course. Can I be like that acorn? Can I keep moving forward, despite the obstacles and challenges, past my parents' worries about my future, and even my own?

As the leaf with its precious cargo disappears under the bridge, a voice in my head scolds, *Where do you get such ridiculous ideas? You, a mere girl, choosing such an unlikely future on untraveled paths? If you keep this up, you will spoil your prospects forever.* But this is not *my* voice. This is the voice of those boys in my drawing class who taunted me. The professors who belittled me. No, *my* voice encourages me onward, toward a future I'm aching to begin.

Standing alone on the bridge, watching the seagulls skim across the lake's rippling surface, I recall a precious moment. Cousin Pierre and I are walking the length of the spectacular Brooklyn Bridge, talking about the smallest details of its construction, sketchbooks in hand. I remember that joyful, hopeful feeling I have hugged close to my heart ever since. My search to make the feeling last forever has only just begun.

EPILOGUE

With her parents' permission to attend Mr. Maybeck's seminar, Julia Morgan began her journey into the creative world of architectural design. Bernard Maybeck, recognizing her potential, invited her to become his intern. Over the next two years they worked together on several projects, during which time Mr. Maybeck continued to encourage Julia to attend the École des Beaux-Arts in Paris. With her parents' agreement, Julia decided to try.

Julia arranged to travel to Paris, accompanied by her old classmate Arthur Brown, who also planned to study architecture at the École. His mother would join them and help Arthur set up his apartment. The perfect plan, until Mrs. Brown took sick at the last minute. Julia knew her parents would not allow her to travel abroad unattended, but a note from Jessica Peixotto changed everything. Jessica was also heading to Paris to study economics at the Sorbonne University. In June 1896, Jessica and Julia became travel companions, first by train then by boat.

Finally, in February 1902, after six grueling years and challenging circumstances, Julia succeeded in becoming the first woman accepted by the École to study architecture—and upon completing the program, she became the first woman to earn a certificate. Before her return home, the *Oakland Tribune* headline trumpeted:

OAKLAND GIRL
BECOMES ARCHITECT IN PARIS

Two years later she became the first woman in California to be granted an architect's license. Between 1902 and 1947, she created and supervised the construction of more than 700 structures, an average of fifteen every year. By contrast, Bernard Maybeck, her friend and mentor, completed an average of roughly two buildings a year.

In the 1930s, Morgan bought a Spanish-style bungalow in the forested hills overlooking Monterey Bay, where she added a work studio. In this place she created a hideaway for herself—a place to draw, read, hike, and rejuvenate from work's heavy demands. She died at the age of eighty-seven. Fifty-seven years after her passing, in 2014, Julia Morgan became the first female architect to receive the American Institute of Architect's highest honor—the Gold Medal Award.

AUTHOR'S NOTE

L ittle is known about Julia Morgan's personal life, especially her early years. Throughout her life, she fiercely guarded her privacy. In fact, she liked to say that if you wanted to know about her, look at her buildings—the homes, the churches, the castles.

Born in the suffocating Victorian era when girls were routinely denied access to education, Julia refused to follow the path that her comfortable upbringing decreed—to marry and raise a family. Few women chose career over marriage. Julia chose architecture, then a male profession, and despite all odds, she succeeded. In *Drawing Outside the Lines*, I create a plausible story about the beginning of her unlikely, challenging journey.

With so little known about her youth, I identified key historical events that would have intersected with her life, such as the completion of the Brooklyn Bridge in 1883 or the World's Fair of 1893. The result is a story that blends nonfiction with fiction, curiosity with imagination. Inevitably, Julia Morgan's story engaged my heart and mind.

THE FIVE MORGAN SIBLINGS

A rare set of letters from the Julia Morgan Collection at California Polytechnic State University offers a vivid picture of a brief but important period when six-year-old Julia stayed at her grandmother's home in Brooklyn. Written by Julia's mother (Eliza Morgan) to her father (Charles B. Morgan) during a temporary separation, the letters describe the personalities of the young Morgan siblings, except for Sam, born a few years later. These descriptions helped me create Julia's family story.

In these letters we learn that young Julia is considerate, observant, cooperative, a little uncoordinated, small, and thin. However, when facing terrible pain, the girl could lash out and fight back with astonishing strength for one so tiny.

We learn that Parmelee, from an early age, has the makings of a rascal. We know he generally misbehaves when visiting his aunt's house, and that he bullies his sisters. Emma is described as intelligent, "cool and calculating," and possessing a quick temper. Avery, often described as an irritable two-year-old, rarely earns a good word from his mother.

As the Morgan children grow into adults, the thread of these early characteristics persists. Parmelee Morgan, a man with little ambition, maintains a distant relationship with his family. He eventually marries and settles in Los Angeles, changing jobs several times. He dies at forty-seven, leaving behind a young wife and five-year-old daughter.

Emma graduates from Berkeley's University of California, and ten years after meeting Hart Wyatt North, they finally marry. Early in their marriage Emma enrolls in San Francisco's Hastings School of Law where she earns a degree in law. Hart North is elected to a California legislative office. Due to Emma's heart condition from childhood scarlet fever, she is advised against having children. Naturally, she ignores the advice, bearing one son. She also keeps her law license current until her death at the age of ninety-six.

Ornery Avery turns into an agreeable adult, though subject to depression. He follows his sisters to the University of California at Berkeley where he studies civil engineering, then travels to Paris to live with Julia where he, too, studies architecture. He doesn't adapt well, soon returning to Oakland where he lives in the family home for several years. Like his older brother Parmelee, Avery frequently changes jobs, never holding one for more than a few years. Despite the many low points in his life, he remains close to his older sister, Julia. He dies at sixty-seven.

Sam, the youngest Morgan, eventually becomes a fireman, so it was an easy stretch to portray him as an excited six-year-old watching Oakland High School burn—twice! At eighteen and still in high school, Sam volunteers in the Oakland fire company, sometimes responding to three fires in a single night. He establishes a moving and storage company and also stays active in the fire department, advancing to the rank of Assistant Fire Chief. At thirty-two Sam is severely injured when his fire department roadster collides with a streetcar, ejecting him and his driver from the car. He breaks his jaw, suffers internal injuries as well as a partially torn scalp, dying six months later.

Much has been written about Julia Morgan, the architect. In *Drawing Outside the Lines*, we get a glimpse of the young girl's drive, abilities, and brilliance. As an adult, she forges a trailblazing career with a lifetime of "firsts," which include becoming the first woman to win admission to and complete the architecture program at the École des Beaux-Arts in Paris. Returning to California, she becomes the first woman in the state granted an architect's license. Her career is long, legendary, and prolific.

Career had always been central in her life. At seventy-nine, she reluctantly closed her office, passing away six years later at the age of eighty-five. Almost sixty years later in 2014, the American Institute of Architecture awarded Julia Morgan the Gold Medal, their highest honor and the first to a woman.

INFLUENTIAL PEOPLE IN JULIA'S LIFE

Several individuals influenced Julia's decision to pursue architecture, all of whom you have met—her father, Charles B. Morgan; Mrs. Phoebe Apperson Hearst; her high school mechanical arts teacher, Miss Mollie E. Connors; as well as architects Pierre LeBrun and Bernard Maybeck. I also include her mother, Eliza Woodland Morgan. We know that the adult Julia had a close relationship with her mother, visiting frequently despite her demanding career. The tension between mother and daughter described in *Drawing Outside the Lines* is a combination of a teenage rebellion and author imagination. Mrs. Morgan was always proud of her daughter's achievements despite her life choices.

Miss Connors was a beloved and inspiring teacher for hundreds of Oakland High School students. Many entered careers in engineering and architecture, like Arthur Brown, who became a successful San Francisco architect. Miss Connors inspired many young women like Julia, always eager to recognize their potential and offer support.

Pierre LeBrun's (1846–1924) letters to Julia are my invention, however the idea grew from an actual correspondence between the two that may have started during her college years, continuing throughout his lifetime. In 1909, he completed his most famous commission, a fifty-story tower for the headquarters of the Metropolitan Life Insurance Company in New York's Madison Square. For this achievement, his firm earned an award from the American Institute of Architects for the tallest building in the world at the time of its completion.

Bernard Maybeck (1862–1957) championed new ideas about architecture. He believed that, whenever possible, a building should fit into its environment. This idea differed from the Victorian view that a building should stand out from its surroundings, adorned with as many wooden gingerbread cutouts as possible. When Julia returned from Paris, she collaborated with Maybeck on several projects. He was best known for the way he combined modern materials with traditional forms. Much of his work was destroyed by fire and other natural disasters. When he died at age ninety-five (four months prior to Julia's passing), he was considered an architectural genius of international importance.

REAL LIFE CHARACTERS
Mary McLean is a fascinating person from Julia Morgan's past. Although both girls grew up in Oakland at the

same time, they were not childhood best friends. Their friendship undoubtedly took root in college as fraternity sisters in Kappa Alpha Theta. Julia was indeed a charter member of Theta's Omega chapter, and yes, they referred to KAT as a fraternity then and now.

Fortunately, Mary possessed an exceptional memory of growing up in Oakland. At ninety, she shared those memories in a remarkable interview with the Bancroft Library at the University of California. She described in amazing detail those thrilling fence walks, tree climbs, and details of The Ladies' Room on campus. As I read her story, I realized that a friendship between Julia and McLean offered the perfect vehicle for incorporating her stories into a believable childhood for Julia.

After graduating college, Mary McLean became Dean of Women at Pomona College in Southern California where she also taught English literature and Latin. At twenty-six she married Warren Olney, Jr. who would become a California Supreme Court judge. His father was the mayor of Oakland from 1903–1905, and his sister was another member of Kappa Alpha Theta. And yes, Julia did eventually design a house for her friend Mary.

Most of the other characters in *Drawing Outside the Lines* did overlap in Julia's life, including Augustus Valentine Saph, Arthur Brown, Thomas Taylor, Sheffield Sanford, the Kappa Alpha Theta members, teachers, and professors, and even the custodian Jimmie Tait. Imagination filled in the blank spaces.

The principal at Tompkins Grammar School is briefly mentioned, but he played his own role in history. Do you remember when Mr. Morgan told his family about him?

"Name's Edwin Markham. I hear he's a poet, too. Nice chap."

Shortly after the uproar over sending Oakland pupils to Tompkins Grammar School, Edwin Markham published "The Man with the Hoe," a poem that made him an overnight sensation, and he was acclaimed as one of America's great poets.

Gertrude Stein (1874-1946), who makes a brief appearance as Julia's partner during the high school tandem bike excursion, became a celebrated writer, poet, and art collector. The bike outing and Stein's participation did occur; however Julia's participation is imagined.

Jessica Blanche Peixotto (1864–1941), eight years Julia's senior, was the daughter of a prominent San Francisco family. Thanks to Frank Norris's success in persuading her father to allow Jessica to attend college, Peixotto enrolled at Berkeley in 1891, graduating with the illustrious class of 1894. Two years later she and Julia traveled to Paris together to study—Julia at the École des Beaux-Arts and Jessica at the Sorbonne University. Upon her return, Jessica earned a PhD at UC Berkeley, the second doctorate awarded to a woman in the college's history. In 1904 she joined the Department of Economics and later became the first woman faculty member to achieve the rank of full professor in 1918. The classes she taught eventually grew into the Department of Social Welfare. Three years after her death, that department became the School of Social Welfare.

Frank Norris, author of the farce starring Jessica Peixotto as well as the script for Julia's graduation class of 1894 pageant, also went on to become a well-known literary figure. When he died in 1904 at the age of thirty-two, he had already established a national reputation as a respected writer who knew how to enjoy life.

The eucalyptus grove Ben Weed discovered and used for the class of '94's graduation pageant had a surprising destiny. Less than ten years later in 1903, Phoebe Hearst's son, William Randolph Hearst, donated money to transform that grove into the Greek Theater, a large outdoor amphitheater still in use today. During this time, Julia, newly returned from Paris, was working in John Galen Howard's office, the supervising architect for the Berkeley campus. Of all his employees, Julia was the best prepared to handle the concrete construction of the Greek Theater, a project plagued by challenges and delays. Amid this chaos, the university decided to hold spring graduation ceremonies there. The invited speaker was none other than President Theodore Roosevelt. Julia had to transform this unfinished amphitheater into a site that would properly honor the president of the United States. In order to create the impression of completed structures, she supervised the building of temporary wooden frames for a speaker's platform, which she then covered with colorful banners and endless yards of muslin. It was a huge success.

While most of the characters in *Drawing Outside the Lines* were based on real people, there is a notable exception—Mary's high school heartthrob, George Tuttle. His character is based on two interesting facts. First, it was not unusual for students to travel great distances to attend Oakland High School and to reside with local families. Established in 1868, Oakland High was the sixth public high school in California, earning an early reputation for academic excellence. Secondly, Mary's father, Pastor McLean of the First Congregational Church, regularly welcomed missionaries from around the world into the McLean home.

AND SO. . .

Julia Morgan battled gender discrimination her entire life. The 19th Amendment granting all American women the right to vote was finally ratified on August 18, 1920. By then Julia was thirty-nine years old and had established a successful architectural firm. Julia Morgan persisted, undeterred by obstacles that would discourage most.

She applied her engineering know-how of reinforced concrete to hundreds of projects, providing them with remarkable resilience. I wonder if Professor Soulé could have ever imagined such an amazing future for the petite, soft-spoken, brilliant woman who stood before him in his engineering class so long ago.

ACKNOWLEDGMENTS

B ooks are a collaborative affair. Even though I work in isolation, I am hardly alone. So many amazing people have played a role in the creation of *Drawing Outside the Lines*. At the top of the list are SparkPress publisher Brooke Warner and Editorial Project Manager Lauren Wise whose belief in this book—as well as their stellar expertise, support, and enthusiasm—made it happen. Special acknowledgement to SparkPress art director Julie Metz and cover designer Lindsey Cleworth for creating the knock-out cover, and designer Tabitha Lahr for the impeccable interior design.

I am also grateful to Suzanna Klein for her charming drawings of significant buildings from Julia Morgan's early years. Sadly, none of those structures are standing today, but Suzanna's work beautifully brings them back to life.

Books that fictionalize a real person's life must be carefully researched and deemed plausible. Fortunately, Karen McNeill PhD, a Julia Morgan scholar, agreed to read early drafts with her expert historian's eye. Her support and input have been indispensable and deeply appreciated.

215

Thanks as well to Laura Sorvetti, Reference Librarian for Special Collections and Archives at the Kennedy Library, Cal Poly, San Luis Obispo. Other invaluable research sources include the University of California Bancroft Library Special Collections, the Oakland Public Library History Collection, art historian Sarah Gill, and educators Margit McGuire PhD and Bettie Luke.

I am also indebted to my editor, Catherine Frank, who guided me through the maze of possibilities with patience and skill, to Laura Atkins for her spot-on editor's eye for story, and to my copyeditor, Jennifer Pellman, whose careful read made the manuscript sparkle.

A shout-out to my fellow writers who listened, supported, and encouraged me during the past eight years: Susan Nunes Fadley, Diane De Pisa, Mary Parks, Kaye Sharon, Joan Matronarde, Dorty Nowak, Mary Heller, and all the members of the Berkeley Writer's Workshop, my own Greek chorus. Thanks as well to Burl Willes for his unwavering support.

I am fortunate to have a family who has always been there for me, cheering me on. I would not have been able to complete this book without Molly and Kim's careful read of each of my "last drafts" or Mike's boundless confidence in me.

And finally, a deep bow of gratitude to Julia Morgan for showing me that drawing "outside the lines" takes tons of courage and a good dose of persistence.

ABOUT THE AUTHOR

Author and educator Susan Austin loves writing historical fiction for young readers, crafting stories that bring alive bygone eras. Her books feature characters who are almost always brave, persistent, and willing to take risks. *The Bamboo Garden*, set in Berkeley, California, 1923, is about an unlikely friendship that is tested by a fierce fire threatening to destroy their town. Currently, she is working on a story set in 1920 Hollywood, starring twelve-year-old Goldie whose talent in the kitchen just might help get her family's delicatessen out of a pickle.

Austin lives in Northern California, in a storybook bungalow surrounded by fruit trees, fussy rose bushes, and a plethora of birds. If you happen to walk by on a nice day, you might see her writing from the comfort of her front porch, coffee mug by her side. Learn more about the author at www.susanjaustin.com.

Author photo © Laura Turbow

SELECTED TITLES FROM SPARKPRESS

SparkPress is an independent boutique publisher delivering high-quality, entertaining, and engaging content that enhances readers' lives, with a special focus on female-driven work. www.gosparkpress.com

The House Children: A Novel, Heidi Daniele. $16.95, 978-1-943006-94-6. A young girl raised in an Irish industrial school accidentally learns that the woman she spends an annual summer holiday with is her birth mother.

The Leaving Year: A Novel, Pam McGaffin. $16.95, 978-1-943006-81-6. As the Summer of Love comes to an end, 15-year-old Ida Petrovich waits for a father who never comes home. While commercial fishing in Alaska, he is lost at sea, but with no body and no wreckage, Ida and her mother are forced to accept a "presumed" death that tests their already strained relationship. While still in shock over the loss of her father, Ida overhears an adult conversation that shatters everything she thought she knew about him. This prompts her to set out on a search for the truth that takes her from her Washington State hometown to Southeast Alaska.

The Forbidden Temptation of Baseball, Dori Jones Yang. $12.95, 978-1-943006-32-8. Twelve-year-old Leon is among a group of 120 boys sent to New England in the 1870s by the Emperor of China as part of a Chinese educational mission. Once there, he falls in love with baseball, even though he's expressly forbidden to play. The boy's host father, who's recently lost his own son in an accident, sees and cultivates Leon's interest, bringing joy back into his own life and teaching Leon more about America through its favorite sport than any rule-bound educational mission could possibly hope to achieve.

Crumble: A Novel, Fleur Philips. $15, 978-1-94071-611-4. Eighteen-year-old Sarah Mcknight has a secret. She's in love with David Brooks. Sarah is white. David is black. But Sarah's not the only one keeping secrets in the close-knit community of Kalispell, Montana.

But Not Forever: A Novel, Jan Von Schleh. $16.95, 978-1-943006-58-8.When identical fifteen-year-old girls are mysteriously switched in time, they discover the love that's been missing in their lives. Torn, both want to go home, but neither wants to give up what they now have.

The Frontman:A Novel, Ron Bahar. $16.95, 978-1-943006-44-1. During his senior year of high school, Ron Bahar—a Nebraskan son of Israeli immigrants—falls for Amy Andrews, a non-Jewish girl, and struggles to make a career choice between his two other passions: medicine and music.